THE TROUBLE WITH TINSEL

KELLY COLLINS

BOOK NOOK PRESS

For all the elves in my life. You are the sparkle on my pine cones, and the tinsel on my tree.

CHAPTER ONE

MANDY

Tommy lounged sleepy-eyed in front of the television as I whisper-yelled at my mother. "You lied to me." Frustration blazed through me like dry kindling set afire. "You said you fell and broke your arm, and here you sit, decorating cookies?"

Unrepentant, Mom gripped the icing bag in her left hand while her bandaged right wrist sat on the table. "I didn't lie. I slipped on the ice. I thought I'd broken my hand." She dropped the bag, tugged at the binding, and tightened the clip. "It was a serious sprain, Mandy."

I'd do anything for my mother, but I was tired of being manipulated—of people stealing my choices—and my mother was the queen of doing that. All my life, she'd cajoled and nudged, pushing me in the direction that benefited her most. Just when I thought she'd changed...

"I dragged Tommy across the country for a sprain?" I stomped to the old percolator. It burped and spit on the counter while I poured a fresh cup. I needed caffeine, and Mom needed to move into the present. The past wasn't a place I wanted to dwell upon or repeat.

Cloves, and cinnamon, and hope filled the air. Mom sat at the table and dressed the gingerbread men in white icing pants and button-down vests, with delicate, precise movements. When I was a little girl, those scents would dare me to dream that my mother would be like everyone else's mom—that I would walk in the door and she'd want nothing more than to hug me and ask me how I was. But that wasn't the game my mother played. Every smile, every cookie, was a bargaining chip—a way to get me to bend to her will. Yet, here I was, hoping all over again, like a kid who couldn't give up on Santa.

In all honesty, she couldn't help herself. She'd clung to whatever control she could since Daddy died.

"Mom." The hours of travel had roughened my voice. "You called me in tears telling me to come home, the shop would perish without me." I waved my hands through the air as I spoke. I didn't usually act with such flair, but Mom had made it sound like her world would implode without me.

"I can't run the shop with this on my hand." She pulled at the elastic bandage again and sighed. "Besides, it was time for you to come home. You hate New York."

A fact she'd been trying to convince me of since I moved there. "I don't hate New York, Mom." I didn't hate the city; I was indifferent to it. It served its purpose —it was far away from Bell Mountain and it held my job.

In retrospect, being here for two weeks would be a

nice respite, but I'd never allow my mother to own that victory.

Mom traded the white icing bag for the red and squeezed out perfect little buttons on the tiny vests. "Bell Mountain is the perfect place to raise my grandson," she whispered, ignoring what I said. She lifted her gaze in Tommy's direction and gave him a nod.

The legs of the chair squeaked as I pulled it from the table and flopped onto the cracked, red vinyl cushion. Mom was stuck in the decade she was born with her diner décor and black and white checkered flooring. Stuck was something I was familiar with. I hadn't been living my dream. I'd been living in New York and working as a pastry chef for Henry Lefebvre, or as I like to call him, Ornery, and that was no dream. My dreams had died the day a certain man walked out of my life.

Sipping my coffee, I glanced around the kitchen. Nailed to the walls were records by Buddy Holly, Chubby Checkers, and the king himself, Elvis Presley. The chipped jar I painted in fourth grade sat in the corner next to the stove overflowing with utensils. My elementary school pictures were still taped to the side of the refrigerator. No matter how far I strayed, how crazy she drove me, or how long I stayed away, this would always be home. "You're right, Tommy will love it here, but this isn't permanent. It's just to get you through the holidays." I grabbed the white icing bag from the plate and helped her with the cookies. It was time to let go of my annoyance, and embrace the holiday spirit. Tonight, we were going to decorate the Christmas tree together for the first time since Tommy was born.

"You used to love Bell Mountain too, sweetheart. Everything you could ever want is here." Mom cupped my cheek with her bandaged hand. Her eyes lit up with love.

Not everything, Mom. Bell Mountain had broken me ten years ago when Beau Tinsel left town with his guitar and my heart.

———

Whoever said picking out a Christmas tree was fun, never did it in subzero weather. Cloudy puffs of steam escaped my mouth each time I breathed. "What about this one?" My teeth chattered while I yanked down Tommy's hat to cover his reddened ears.

Mom, Tommy, and I stood in front of the tree and analyzed it from all angles. "Can't we have a flucked one, Mommy?" Tommy pointed at the tent where a man was glazing a perfect green tree in spongy white material. The fake snow glittered like diamonds under the fluorescent lights.

"It's called flocked, and no, we can't. All white trees belong outside." Surrounded by naturally snow-coated trees, it was overkill to bring a poser into the house. "If you want, we can decorate the pine tree in Grandma's front yard, too. Then you can have a white and a green tree."

My little man jumped up and down with the energy only a child can possess and maintain. "This one's super-duper then."

An uncontainable shiver raced from the tip of my

head all the way to my boots. I looked toward my mother, praying she would give her seal of approval before any part of me froze and dropped off. "Okay with you, Mom?"

Mom rounded the tree again. Tommy and I watched as she analyzed each full branch and prickly needle. Just when I thought she'd put a kibosh on it, she smiled and said, "super-duper with me, too. I'll pay." She turned and walked toward the man at the front of the lot.

"Mandy Sawyer?"

I recognized his voice right away. It was pure warmth. "Greg Anderson, how the heck are you?" I wrapped my arms around the boy who'd been my Godsend the last year of high school. We'd stayed in touch for a time, but eventually, I found it easier to sever as many ties with my past as I could. "You're still here?"

Stepping back, I looked at him. He was tall, handsome, and totally not into girls. In fact, Greg Anderson came out on prom night. He was my date, and we had arrived at the dance wearing matching pink gowns. It was a testament to our friendship and a show of solidarity. The fact he had looked better in the dress than I did should have pissed me off, but I could never get angry with Greg. He had been the best boy friend a girl could ever have. And, he was the perfect prom date. He paid for his own dinner and didn't expect to get lucky in the back seat of his car when the night ended.

He opened his arms with a flourish and looked around him. "I couldn't leave all this behind." He kneeled down in front of Tommy. "And who's this handsome young man?"

Pride radiated from my pores. "This is my son, Tommy." Tommy stared up at Greg and smiled like he was looking into the face of an angel. Greg had that effect on everyone. Something wonderful and happy arrived each time he did. He was hot chocolate on a frigid day and fuzzy socks on a cold morning. He was one of those feel-good people.

"Tommy, this is my friend, Greg."

Tommy offered his hand, "I'm Tommy Sawyer, it's nice to meet you." For a six-year-old, he was already a charmer. I'd have to keep an eye on him. With his devilish good looks and charisma, he was bound to break the hearts of many.

Greg raised a single brow in question. "Tom Sawyer? You didn't really do that to him, did you?"

"Do what to me, Mommy?" Tommy looked at me with saucer-sized eyes.

"I named you after a famous character from a book." I gave Greg a little push and a shut-the-hell-up look.

He rose to a towering height and whispered in my ear. "You better teach him to fight."

My mouth dropped open. "Never. He'll be fine. It's character-building."

"Whatever you say." Amusement glinted in his eyes. "Where's his dad?" Greg scanned the tree lot as if looking for someone in particular.

"My dad is famous and very busy," Tommy piped in.

"Is that right?" Greg raised his hand for a high-five. "Right on." He turned to me with an inquisitive tilt to his head.

"No, it's not who you think. It's a long story that's better left for coffee, a pastry, and a warmer environment. What about tomorrow at the Sweet Shop? I'm filling in for Mom over the holidays." It felt funny to think I'd be running the Sweet Shop but oddly comforting as well. Maybe Mom was right; maybe coming home for a while would be good for me.

"I'll be there around four, and I want every sordid detail."

We hugged once more and parted. Despite my misgivings about coming home, the comfort of old friends was encouraging.

After we hefted the tree to the roof of my Jeep, we were on our way. Thankfully, I kept the old heap of junk. It was covered and waiting in the garage for me when I got back into town. After sitting for nearly a decade, it turned over on the first try, proving that not everything from the past would fail me.

Once home, I muscled the tree through the front door. A gimpy mother and a little boy weren't much help, but they tried, and I appreciated their efforts. The tree fit perfectly in front of the window, and while I fluffed out the branches, Mom and Tommy sifted through what he called "big CD's." Moments later, the sound of Bing Crosby was crackling and popping on the record player. No digital for Mom. She was old school.

They went into the kitchen to make cocoa while I pulled the old boxes of Christmas decorations up from the basement. Decorating the tree would be a walk down memory lane. Mom never got rid of anything. Whereas she was married to the past, I'd hurled myself into the future, leaving everything behind.

"Are you two ready?" I called from the living room once the lights had been hung from the tree.

"On our way," Mom sang from the kitchen. There was a bit of banging and a lot of giggling coming from their direction, then two elves appeared wearing green and red striped hats and pointed foam ears. The littlest elf carried a plate of gingerbread cookies while the older, supposedly more mature elf brought hot cocoa. A smile lifted my lips. It had been a long time since I'd seen my mom participate in anything joyful. "You two are the cutest in the world." I wiggled Tommy's little nose and told him he got to choose the first ornament for the tree.

He went straight for the homemade decorations. A bejeweled pine cone swung from his little fingers. He held it up and asked who made it. If every ornament needed an explanation, it would be a long night.

"That one was made by your mom with her best friend, Beau. They sat right here in this living room and glued glitter to pine cones. On small pieces of paper, they wrote their secret wishes and tucked them between the scales where they stayed until Christmas morning." Mom was like Dickens; she held the power to mesmerize an audience with the way she weaved a story. Tommy was not immune and his eyes grew wide with curiosity.

"What was your secret wish?" he asked as he hung

the glittered pine cone from a center bow. It shimmered under the twinkling lights.

"I can't remember," I fibbed. I remembered exactly what I wished for. I was ten and Beau was eleven. In my best cursive, I wrote that I wanted to grow up and marry Beau Tinsel.

"Of course you remember. How could you forget? That's the one that said you wanted to—"

"Mom!" I stopped her mid-sentence. I didn't want to rehash that memory, and I didn't want to explain Beau to Tommy. What was the point in introducing him to my past—a past that had no influence on Tommy or our future? No, Beau Tinsel was a faint memory, at best.

"What? I was going to say that you and Beau had made the sweetest wishes."

"Did your wish come true?" Tommy pulled a gingerbread man from the plate and licked the red buttons from the vest.

"No, Tommy, my wish didn't come true." My shoulders slumped forward with the knowledge that someday, I'd have to tell him that wishes rarely came true, and life could be hard. At his age, everything was still possible.

Mom picked up the next ornament and hung it toward the top. "The beauty about wishes is, they sit out there and wait for the perfect time to come true, Tommy." She gave me a let-him-dream look and I nodded my head in agreement. There was time enough for the cruelties of the world to rain disappointment on him. For now, let him live in his happy child's world.

"Can we do that, Grandma? Can we decorate pine cones and hide wishes?" Tommy pulled a package of tinsel from the box and stared at his Grandma with expectant eyes. "I have a bunch of wishes."

"As soon as we finish this tree, you and I are going pine cone hunting, we'll let them dry overnight and decorate them tomorrow." Mom's grandma skills stood in direct contrast with her mom skills. With Tommy, she was patient and playful. With me, adding an "S" before "mothering" nailed it on the head.

Tommy threw tinsel into the air in celebration. It's sparkly strands showered down on everyone. Even a bit hit the tree. Tommy was having fun and hearing his laughter warmed my heart.

I walked around the tree to the window and wiped the condensation from the pane with my sleeve. The old Victorian across the street stood regal. Its decorative trim and garland-wrapped windows screamed "happy holidays." The icicle lights sparkled like the tinsel on our tree. Through the fogged glass, I reflected on a different time—different Tinsel.

Beau Tinsel had been the love of my life. *Remember me,* he'd said that last night. The next day, he drove away with his guitar in the back seat of his SUV. He headed west and never looked back. That was years ago and my heart still ached.

Mom and Tommy were laughing at the silver strands that decorated the room. The trouble with tinsel was, it was hard to control. It stuck to you or was repelled by you. There was no in-between. It attached to you until something more interesting or electrifying came by. Tinsel was fickle. Tinsel was unpredictable. Tinsel broke my heart.

Mom gathered up the cups from the coffee table when she let it slip. "He's coming back home, you know?"

"Who?" I played stupid. It had been ten years since he'd left, and I hadn't seen him since. The truth was, I'd stalked him on social media, bought every one of his new releases, and even went to a concert when he was performing in New York City.

"Your Beau is coming home. It's time for him, too."

"He's not my Beau, Mom." With my arms crossed over my chest, I asked, "What are you up to?"

"Me?" Her voice swooped low and ended high. She was feigning innocence, but I knew Mom was up to something and if that were the case, Sarah Tinsel was an accomplice. "Did Sarah break her wrist, too?" Beau hadn't come home once since he'd left town. The only thing that would bring him back would be an emergency. I looked heavenward, silently begging her to come clean.

"Oh, heavens no. She twisted her ankle." Mom exited the room laughing.

Hot on her heels, I marched into the kitchen. "Your meddling isn't going to get you anywhere."

"Oh, Mandy, must you act so dramatic. Maybe you missed your calling." She dumped the cups in the sink and proceeded to fill it with hot water and bubbles.

"Mom, you and I both know Beau isn't coming home. He never comes back to Bell Mountain."

"Neither did you, but I got you home." She waved her wounded hand in the air. As usual, not really listening to me. She had already moved on to the next thing. "Tommy, let's go pine cone hunting, and then, you're off to bed, young man. Your mother volunteered to clean the kitchen while we search."

They wrapped themselves in winter gear and disappeared out the back door, leaving me alone with unwelcome thoughts of Beau. If all it took was a twisted ankle to get him back, I should have faked an injury long ago. Sadly, too much time had passed, and our lives had irrevocably changed. He was a star, and I was a single mother. And whatever we might have had between us died a long time ago. I had moved on, moved away from Beau. Still, there were days when the loss weighed heavy on me.

I twisted a piece of tinsel around my finger until the tip turned purple and throbbed. I remembered that feeling well, although last time, I felt it in my heart. Losing Beau was like slowly being suffocated.

For a moment, I stood by the window and watched the house across the street. *Where have you been, Beau Tinsel? Are you really coming home?*

I turned away from the window and curled up in the overstuffed chair next to the over-decorated tree and sipped my orange, spiced tea. Too many days had been spent in this chair waiting for Beau to return. Too many days wishing for something that would never happen.

Today, I sat and hoped he'd stay away.

CHAPTER TWO

BEAU

It was well after midnight when I pulled in front of my childhood home. Everything looked the same and yet, it wasn't. Ten years was a long time, but the memories of loving and leaving Mandy were too painful to face, so I stayed away—far away.

Mom had outdone herself this year, or maybe this was how it was every year. I couldn't be sure. Icicle lights hung from the rooftop, illuminating the intricate details of the house. Garland wrapped the windows and framed the red door while a wreath welcomed me back. Over a hundred years old, the home had weathered its ups and downs much better than I had.

As soon as Mom had called and told me she'd fallen down the stairs, I hopped on the first plane out of Los Angeles and headed home. Home…It was an odd feeling to be back in the place where I gained and lost so much.

Once out of the SUV, my eyes gravitated to one place—Mandy's house. She used to sit in that window and wait for me. It was as dark and vacant as my heart. I heard she was happy, living in New York with her family. It crushed me to think of her with anyone else, but her happiness was all I ever wanted.

"Beau, come on in honey. I've been waiting for you." Mom stood on the front porch wrapped in her blue bathrobe. She was crutch free, cast free, and cane free, which meant she wasn't guilt free. I had a mind to trip her just to make an honest woman out of her. "I'll make cocoa." She spun on her perfectly stable feet and hurried inside the house.

One last look in Mandy's direction was all I'd allow myself for now. With my suitcase in one hand and my guitar in the other, I walked toward the door. Even though ten years had passed, the thought of her gripped my chest.

Walking in the house was like being sucked through a wormhole and flung back into the past. Except, it went way back to a time when my father was alive and my stepfather never existed. The family portraits, once removed, were back in their place of honor, laid out like a game of solitaire on the entry wall. I'd always thought of them as personal greeters—kind of like visiting Wal-Mart and getting a friendly hello upon entering.

It was almost unfathomable that Bell Mountain came to exist because my great-great-grandfather and his friend, John Grady, walked up an unclaimed mountain shaped like a bell. They had nothing but a pick-ax and a hundred bucks between them when they began to dig. T & G Mine has pulled gold from the backside of Bell Mountain ever since.

After I dumped my stuff in my bedroom, I went in search of Mom. She was singing, "Oh Holy Night," which happened to be my favorite Christmas carol. This was no accident. Mom knew I could never stay angry with her. Her sweet voice had always softened my rough edges and eased me through the tough times. Music was a salve to my wounded soul. It had been, and would always be, my escape.

"You lied to me." I reached over her, kissing her cheek and pulling two mugs from the cupboard, thankful I remembered where they were kept.

"I wanted my son home for the holidays. Desperate times call for desperate measures and all that."

"Did you even fall at all?" I stood to her side and watched her eye twitch while she tapped her foot on the tile floor.

She poured cocoa powder into the steaming milk and stirred. "Well, I stubbed my toe last month. That should count for something."

"Why didn't you just ask me to come home?" I thought of all the times she'd pleaded with me to do just that, but I was never ready to face the truth of everything I'd given up. No, I avoided the past like it was a contagion.

"I've been begging you to come home for years, Beau. The only time I get to see you is when I come to you." She ladled the hot chocolate into the mugs and brought them to the dining room where we took a seat at the antique mahogany table. A large chandelier sparkled overhead and cast prisms of light across the beige and gold fabric that covered the walls. Mandy always loved this room. She said the dining room was the heart of every home. It was where people shared their lives, their hopes, and their dreams.

"I'm sorry, you know how busy I am." I was busy, but I'd hit a level in my career where I controlled everything. Gone were the days when my manager called, and I hopped to do his bidding. After fifteen top-ten hits and two albums that went platinum, I didn't answer to anyone but myself.

"That's bull and you know it," she said, her voice showing signs of agitation that hadn't caught up to her eyes, which were still soft with love.

"It looks like we're both caught in a lie. They say the apple rarely falls far from the tree." I sipped at my hot cocoa and savored the hot liquid as it warmed my insides. Mom never made instant cocoa. She had created her own proprietary blend that was perfect in every way.

Her hand covered mine. "I'm so happy to have you home, Beau." Mom's smile was like looking into the soul of goodness. She'd always done what was best for me, except marrying my stepfather. That was a selfish moment she deserved after years of seeing to my needs.

"I'm sorry it took me so long to come home." I slouched back in the chair and exhaled. "In all honesty, it's hard to come home and be reminded of what I gave up. Then there was your douchebag of a husband."

"Do you have to use that word?" Mom didn't tolerate cussing unless, of course, she was the one blurting out an expletive, and that only happened once to my recollection. The day my father died, the sheriff brought his fishing pole to the door and Mom yelled at him. *"Bring me my husband, not his damn fishing pole."* That day changed a lot of lives.

My dad and Mandy's dad were best friends, our mothers were best friends, and it went without saying Mandy and I were best friends. Ice fishing was a winter must. It was late January and the ice was frozen solid. At least, that's what everyone thought until they fell through. Dad fell in and drowned. Mandy's dad tried to save him and died from hypothermia. That's what friends did for friends. They sacrificed themselves for the benefit of the other. I did that for Mandy, but she didn't have a clue as to how much of a sacrifice it was for me.

"Mom, he was an awful man. Why you stayed with him for so long is beyond me." She married him the year before my graduation. He didn't like anything that diverted my mom's attention away from him, including me.

"He was kind of a douchebag." She smiled over her cup while I choked.

"You did not just say that."

"Say what?" She smiled with feigned innocence. "As for marrying Ted, I was lonely."

"I was here."

"You were always going to leave to chase your dream, and you didn't warm my bed."

"That's just gross, Mom. I don't want to think about you and Ted doing the dirty." Ugh, tremors ran down my body. Knowing she was married to the bastard was bad enough, but imagining they had sex was over the top. I refused to go there.

"Ted married me for my money. I married him so the house wouldn't be so quiet when you left. The pickings are slim in a small town."

"You could have adopted a dog."

She shrugged. "When they come up with a breed that cleans up its poop, I will."

I was on a European tour when Ted passed away last year. I offered to cancel it and come home, but Mom insisted I finish what I started. "When you told me he'd died, I thought maybe you'd come to your senses and pushed him down the stairs. I know I wanted to on several occasions." The man was that awful. He moved in and took over like he owned the place. This house, the mines, and all the other businesses my father and his ancestors had sweat and bled for were not Ted's. They belonged to the Tinsels, and I'd lost all respect for the man when he stopped working after knowing he landed a cash cow by marrying my mother. The only benefit to my mom was people no longer looked at her with sadness in their eyes. The widow Tinsel had found love again. What a bunch of crap.

"He wasn't so bad, just selfish, and his greedy little heart was weak. At least he died doing what he loved. He was at the bank counting his withdrawal when his heart exploded."

"Do you think you'll ever find the kind of love you had with Dad?"

"Oh, I think burying two husbands is enough for a one woman. I'm what you'd call a black widow," she replied with a hint of sass in her voice. "What about you? Are you ever going to patch things up with Mandy?"

When I'd called and told her I wasn't coming home, she broke apart. Her cries still haunted my memories. "She'd never forgive me."

"I almost didn't forgive you. Although misguided, at least your actions were honorable. You need to tell her the truth."

"What's the point? There are too many years between us. I'm not that boy anymore, and she's not the same girl. Didn't you tell me she was married, with a child, and living in New York?"

"Do you ever listen?" Mom reached over and cuffed me upside the head. "She. Is. Not. Married." Her pitch rose and ended on a frustrated screech. "She has a little boy that Annie never stops talking about. I'd like some grandchildren too, by the way." She downed her cocoa like it was a stiff shot of brandy. "She's back in Bell Mountain for the holidays, and if Annie gets her way, she'll be here to stay." Mom looked triumphant in her declaration.

Her words were like a wrecking ball to the side of my head. Mandy was back in Bell Mountain. I was back in Bell Mountain. This could be really good, or it could be really bad.

I narrowed my eyes at her. "What are you and Annie up to?" It was obvious they were in cahoots. Those two were peas from the same pod.

"We aren't up to anything." Mom picked up the empty cups and dismissed me with a wave. "So what if you find yourself at the Sweet Shop tomorrow. So what if Mandy's there, and she's as beautiful and smart as the day you left. So what if you find yourself in love with her again."

Yep, those two were trouble. "So what, huh?" I stood up to follow her.

"Yes, Beau, so what?"

"I hate to break it to you, but nothing is going to happen between Mandy and me."

"Stop being a douchebag, Beau. Pull your head from your ass and start living." Mom stomped into the kitchen and dumped the cups into the sink before she marched off to bed.

Once I picked my jaw up from the floor, I walked to the front window and stared at the little house across the street. Everything seemed the same, only it wasn't. My mom had adopted a potty mouth, and Mandy Sawyer was back home. *Could she ever forgive me?*

CHAPTER THREE

MANDY

The dripping of the faucet kept me awake all night, but it was necessary so the pipes didn't burst when the weather dropped below freezing. After a fitful night of sleep, I woke up late for my first day at the shop. With my hair pulled into a ponytail, I ran down the stairs buttoning up my shirt. Tommy and Mom were already in the kitchen.

"Not too many sweets, and if he starts getting cranky, make him lay down for a bit." I rushed around the kitchen like a strung-out caffeine addict trying to get her next fix.

"It's under control. I raised you, and you survived." She pulled the pancake mix from the cupboard and started to whip up Tommy's breakfast.

"Barely." I stuck my tongue out at her like a juvenile. She grabbed a spatula from the chipped jar and chased me to the back door. The whole time, Tommy watched and giggled. I ducked under her arm and hid behind my son so I could kiss him goodbye. "Bring him by the shop later?"

"Will do, now get." She waved the spatula through the air like it was Harry Potter's wand. By the way Tommy squealed, I expected an incantation and a puff of smoke to burst from the end before I disappeared.

It was impossible not to glance at the Tinsel house on my way out the door. A silver SUV had appeared overnight, and I knew it was Beau. I felt his presence. Maybe it was my imagination, but the air seemed to contain more energy when he was near. Maybe it only happened when we were together. All I knew was I'd spent most of my life loving Beau Tinsel or pining for him. Maybe it was good he was back. At twenty-eight, I had to move on and bury the past, and I couldn't do that without one final word to Beau, but the lone word that came to mind right now was *asshole*.

The Jeep didn't turn over as easily this morning, but it could be because I left it out all night long. At three below zero, not much wanted to start up and go, including me. I backed out of the driveway and headed to work. Nothing much had changed. As I drove through town staring at the same old buildings, I realized I changed more than Bell Mountain.

"Hey, Misty," I called from the door. Misty Lerner worked at the shop for as long as I could remember. It started out as an after school job for her and turned into a career.

She dropped the scoop, wiped her hands on her apron and pulled me in for a quick hug.

"So, your mom got you to come back." She looked

me up and down and smiled her gap-toothed smile. Her parents offered to close the space with braces in high school, but Misty read somewhere that luck flowed through the space, and she didn't want to jinx herself. I wonder if her life had indeed been lucky.

"Manipulated me back home, you mean." I pulled an apron from a hook by the door and wrapped it around my waist.

"It's been a long time." She gripped my hand and twirled me in a circle. "Was your hair always this blonde? And when did you grow boobs?"

I twisted my fingers through my ponytail and looked down at my chest. "Yep, always blonde, but these," I cupped my ample breasts, "are courtesy of motherhood."

"I hate you." She looked down at her flat chest. "I breastfed both of mine, and they sucked the life out of the girls."

"I didn't breastfeed Tommy. I was single parenting it, and I couldn't stop work every two hours to pump, but he seems to have survived, despite my neglect." Thoughts of Tommy always made me feel light and airy. "How's your family?"

"Divorced two years ago. I caught him banging Michelle Steele on my dining room table."

"Oh. My. God. Michelle? Really?" Michelle was one of the many M names so popular in my generation. My graduating class of one hundred and ten kids had twenty-two girls whose names began with an M, but I'd never have guessed that Michelle could have been so

23

bold. She was the preacher's daughter—a mouse of a girl.

"Your mom sent me home at lunchtime because I wasn't feeling well. It was quite a homecoming to arrive and find Michelle looking after my husband's needs, and I'm not talking about his spiritual needs. To this day, she swears I was possessed by a demon. I hit Dan with the same rolling pin I tried to shove up that girl's ass. I'm told he sported a shiner for a week, and Michelle spent the next few days on her knees, only this time in the front pew of her daddy's church."

Maybe Misty should have closed that gap in her teeth after all. While she talked, I set up the large mixer and poured in the ingredients for sugar cookies. Mom had a large order of blue bells for the ski resort up the road.

"What did Dan have to say for himself?" Dan had always been a player. Most of the jocks were. That's why I'd loved Beau so much. He was loyal to a fault. One day, Theresa Platt, the town whore, had stepped in front of him in the parking lot at school and flashed her enormous boobs in his face. He walked past her like he'd never seen them, and then he wrapped his arms around me as if I was the only girl to exist in his world.

I knew he'd gotten an eyeful. In fact, I was pretty sure he was almost blinded by an eraser-hard nipple, but Beau never reacted. Later in the day, he told me boobs followed a grading scale. Her size C cups were average and my A cups were top of the grading chart. If I were graded by the same scale today, I'd score a low D or a high C, at best.

"What could he say? I caught him with his pants down playing bury the wiener. I didn't know what to do, so I called my daddy. He came over and helped Dan pack. He didn't take much, just his clothes and a stack of bills." She shrugged as if she were talking about a faulty item she'd returned. "Dan lives in a trailer park on the other side of the mountain. He works in the mines now. You can't be a police officer when people question your moral compass." Misty's dad was Sheriff Lerner, and I was pretty sure he had shoved Dan's moral compass straight up his ass.

We talked as if ten years hadn't passed. At seven o'clock, we opened the doors and let the old timers in. Some of them had been coming since I was in diapers. They welcomed me back home and took their favorite seats to sip coffee and gossip.

A few times over the next several hours, I overheard my name and Beau's, but I tried to ignore the whispers and stares. It was old news. However, the problem was, small-town residents could breathe new life into old news, and make it fresh again.

Misty iced the cooled sugar cookies. "I hear Beau is back in town. Have you seen him?"

"Nope." I pulled out a warming plate, a non-stick pan, and a bag of chocolate.

"Just nope? I need more than that." She sprinkled the bells with iridescent, blue candy sprinkles. "What happened with you guys?"

"It wasn't meant to be."

"But you're going to see him, right?"

"It's not in my plans." I stirred the chocolate and

grabbed the caramel squares. "Listen, Misty, Beau and I were kids. That was a long time ago."

"I just thought…" She looked up when the bell above the door rang.

"You thought what?" I focused on dipping caramel squares into milk chocolate.

"I *think* you're going to have to change your plans," was all she said before she snapped her mouth shut. In fact, the entire Sweet Shop went mute. Walking in the door was none other than Beau Tinsel and he looked amazing. When had he grown so tall? Was he always so muscular? And that beard, it was the perfect amount of scruff to rosy up a girl's cheeks or possibly her inner thighs. *Oh, I was in big trouble.*

"Oh, look, it's time for my break." Misty tore off her apron and tossed it on the counter. "See you in thirty." She dashed out the door like her ass was on fire.

"Mandy." My name rolled off his tongue like thick molasses. He approached the display case with his hands tucked into the pockets of his pants. He looked me up and down. "Good to see you, candy girl." I used to love when he called me his candy girl. Now, it sounded as fake as saccharin and left a bitter taste in my mouth.

"I'm no longer your candy girl." I swirled a caramel block into the chocolate and set it on wax paper to dry before I approached the counter.

His body language spoke volumes. Those hands in his pockets said, *I'd rather be anywhere but here*, or maybe he'd forgotten his gloves and his hands were cold. When it came to Beau, I was no longer an expert. One thing I was certain of—I didn't know this Beau Tinsel. The man standing in front of me was large, and looming, and lethal.

A plethora of feelings raced through me—intense sadness, jubilation, relief, and rage. Equally fast, one word filtered through my head—*Asshole. Asshole. Asshole.* It was the only word I could process. I came back to Bell Mountain to help Mom. I didn't want a walk down memory lane. It was inevitable that someday we'd run into one another, but why today?

I'd played out this exact scenario a thousand times. Well, not exactly, because in my dreams, I was ten pounds less and dressed to kill. My hair was styled, and my makeup applied with the skill of an artist. I'd come up with something charming or witty to say to him, but today, I was left with two syllables.

"Asshole," I whispered.

"Excuse me?" He leaned forward like he was hard of hearing. Maybe he was, loud music could do that to a person. I could only be so lucky.

I put on a mask of indifference. Lord knows I'd had a lot of practice in Paris. After I became pregnant with Tommy, I had to see his indifferent father daily. I simply pretended he didn't exist. What I didn't acknowledge couldn't hurt me. Could I do the same with Beau? I'd have to try. "Welcome back, Beau. What can I get you?" I dusted off the already-spotless counter in front of me, anything to distract myself from looking into his sapphire blue eyes. I tugged and pulled at my T-shirt and jeans, hoping I didn't look like the tired mom I'd become. I wanted Beau to see me as the one who got away. I wanted him to regret what he did to me. Sadly,

27

after seeing me today, he'd probably thank his lucky stars.

"Coffee and a banana nut muffin, please."

"Still take it with half a cow and a teaspoon of sugar?" His damn lips curled into a hint of a smile. Boy, even his lips had matured. Were they always that full? Raspberry red? Kissable?

"You remembered." He reached up and plucked a chocolate-covered candy cane from the jar on the counter and gave me a knowing smile.

Those had been our brainchild. It happened on our first kiss. I'd just devoured a peppermint candy and Beau a handful of chocolate kisses when somehow our lips and tongues found each other. I wasn't sure if it was the kiss or the candy that made it sweet and special, but we persuaded my mom to dip canes in chocolate and sell them at the store as a symbol of our love. Whenever I saw them, I thought of our first kiss. *Asshole.*

I did my best to ignore him while I punched his items into the register. It was another old relic from days long past. At one time, this store had been a mercantile that supplied the miners and their families with things like sugar, and flour, and bolts of fabric. My family had a long history with Bell Mountain. Great Grandpa Sawyer worked as a foreman for Old Man Grady. Grady never married, which was a shame because he had the second biggest house in town after the Tinsels. Every time I walked by the Grady house, I tossed a penny in the pond out front and wished someday it would be mine. That wish didn't come true, either.

"Mandy?" His voice worked its way through the haze of my daydream.

I shook my head to clear the thoughts that addled my brain. "Sorry. That will be four dollars and twenty-eight cents."

He handed me a five. "Can we sit down and talk sometime?" His tone was earnest—so much like the young boy I'd fallen in love with, but that boy had gone to California, and I didn't know the man who had returned. He appeared to be the same, but how could he be? He was a superstar. His talent had earned him millions of dollars. No, I didn't know this man, and I couldn't afford to know him. He was dangerous to my heart and soul.

"Yeah, sure, but it will have to wait until after the holidays. Being a candy shop and bakery, you can imagine how busy we are right before Christmas." I gave myself an internal high five. I'd pulled that right out of my patootie. I'd managed to sound indifferent and unfazed even though my throat was in my stomach, and my heart was at my feet.

"I won't be here after the holidays, so maybe you can try to fit me into your busy schedule." He lifted his brows in question.

"Just like you did me?" He irked me, but I disappointed myself with my pettiness. I didn't want to be the scorned girl he'd left behind. I'd grown up, hadn't I? "I'm sorry. That just slipped."

His smile never made it to his eyes. "I deserved that." He picked up his coffee and muffin and walked to a corner table where he sat and stared at me until a gaggle of girls noticed him and began asking him for autographs and pictures. Then, it was my turn to watch.

He didn't appear to relish the attention. He smiled and chatted, but there was no spark in his voice, and no light in his eyes. To the average person, he appeared friendly and engaged, but each time another girl showed up to his table, I could almost hear his sigh of defeat. To his credit though, he posed for pictures and kissed the cheeks of every teen who came to the shop. I was exhausted for him.

When he saw his chance to escape, he made his way toward the door, but not before calling over his shoulder. "It's good to see you, Mandy. You know where to find me."

The bell above the door rang before Beau could exit. My son rushed in like an out of control storm. His arms were full of packages. Lego's, crayons, and paper airplanes littered the ground in his wake.

Beau stepped back when Tommy ran at me, nearly toppling me with his show of robust affection. "Mommy, look at what Grandma bought me."

I glanced over Tommy's shoulder and gave my mom the stink eye. In a matter of days, my once polite, and charming son would be a spoiled brat if I didn't rein her in. I mouthed the words, "no more," then I turned toward my beautiful boy. "Wow, it looks like you had an early Christmas, buddy." I tousled his dark hair.

Beau backed away from the door. His eyes narrowed as he approached and kneeled in front of Tommy. "Hi, I'm Beau, and who are you?"

"I know who you are. You're that man that's on my

mommy's CDs. You sing that song that makes her cry."
Tommy scrunched his nose and pursed his lips.

"Tommy, where are your manners?" I was mortified
that he'd spilled my secrets. How was I supposed to feign
indifference when he'd publicly outed me as a fan? A
blubbering mess of a fan with a bunch of BT and the
Bads CDs. Beau didn't need to know I was a step away
from crazy stalker.

My head dropped in defeat. What could I expect
from a six-year-old if not honesty? "This is Beau, and he
is indeed the lead singer of BT and the Bads."

Tommy held out his hand for a shake. "Nice to meet
you, Beau. Are you really famous?"

Beau's eyes skimmed Tommy from head to toe. His
expression held a thousand questions. "I suppose I am,
but to you, I'm just Beau, and we're going to be friends.
Okay?"

Tommy smiled a rainbow. "Are you my daddy?"

I sucked in my breath while my heart tumbled to the
floor. Tommy had been asking about his dad a lot lately,
and I'd told him his dad was famous and busy. I wasn't
ready to tell him his dad wanted nothing to do with him,
so I embellished the truth. His dad was famous. In fact,
he was one of the premier chocolatiers in Europe, but
he wasn't interested in being a father, and I wasn't interested in an abortion. We parted amicably.

To his credit, Beau didn't blink an eye. "How old are
you, son?" He glanced at me with accusation in his eyes.
Tommy was tall for his age and could have easily passed
for an older boy, but he wasn't Beau's.

"I'm six and a half. Come sit with me and Grandma,

she promised me a cookie." Tommy tugged Beau over to the table he'd just vacated. "Are you my daddy?" he repeated.

After doing the math, Beau had to know Tommy wasn't his, but there was no relief in his expression. In fact, he almost seemed disappointed. "No, Tommy, I'm not your daddy, but if I were, I'd be so proud to call you my son." In that moment, my iciness toward Beau thawed a bit.

The afternoon rush hit. Mom jumped in to run the register with her good hand while Misty and I helped the line of customers. In the corner, Tommy and Beau colored and assembled paper airplanes that often found their way flying over the counter. At four o'clock on the dot, Greg walked in. He was quick to take in the scene. He tossed his head toward the corner table where Beau and Tommy sat. I knew exactly what he was thinking. It was written all over his pretty boy face. *You and Beau are back together?*

I shook my head and mouthed the word, "No." Mom left me at the register to help Greg while she stepped into the back room.

Greg flagged me over to where he stood and something odd happened in that moment. My penis-loving pal gave hetero a try. He reached across the counter, grabbed me by the shirt, and pulled me to him. When he covered my mouth with his lips, I was too stunned to react. The kiss was over as quickly as it began, and for the second time today, the Sweet Shop was silenced.

"I missed you, baby," Greg announced loud enough

for the world to hear. Then, he nuzzled my neck and whispered, "Just play along."

I jumped back a step and whispered. "What? No, it's not like that."

He looked toward the table where Beau and Tommy sat. Tommy was committed to his coloring book while Beau threw virtual daggers in my direction. Was that jealousy I saw simmering below the surface? Could it be?

"Oh honey, open your eyes." Greg's voice stepped down to a whisper, but his intention was loud and clear. "Let the games begin."

CHAPTER FOUR

BEAU

I'd watched as a man entered the shop and pulled Mandy in for a kiss. It wasn't the kind of kiss a friend gave to a friend. It was a kiss that had purpose. He was claiming territory, and I didn't like it. Those should have been my lips pressed against hers, not his. After all these years, I still wanted her.

"Who's that with your mom?"

Tommy looked up from his red crayon and glanced toward the counter where Mandy and the man were whispering.

"That's Greg."

I sized up Greg. He was tall, clean-shaven, and a nice dresser. Definitely hipster. Not someone I would have pegged for Mandy at all. Ten years had obviously changed her taste in men. As I studied Mandy, I realized the years had been good to her. More than good. She was gorgeous. Her body had always been amazing, but it had matured. Everything was curved in the right places. Her breasts, hips, and ass belonged in the

Sweet Shop. They were delectable and would tempt any man.

"Is he your mom's boyfriend?" The guy looked familiar, but I couldn't place him.

Tommy giggled. "He's a boy, and a friend, so yes, he's a boyfriend."

I ruffled his hair. "You're a silly boy." I turned and watched the couple's body language. Greg leaned in each time he spoke to her. The only people who did that were girlfriends and lovers, and he was no girl.

Watching them gutted me. I couldn't take it anymore. Expecting a call from my agent at five, I had a good excuse to leave.

"Tommy, I've got to go, but I live across the street from your Grandma Annie's. Come on over anytime, and we'll fly these airplanes." I picked up the last paper plane I'd folded, jotted my cell number on the wing, and flew it straight at Mandy. What could one more try hurt? It would be great to have some closure before I left town. The plane flew through the air, bounced off her left breast, and landed on the counter in front of her. Not since I'd pegged her forehead with a spitball in English class had my aim been so perfect.

She looked at the paper, then glared at me, and crumpled the plane into a ball. *Yep, crash and burn.* But I wasn't one to give up. When I'd left Colorado, I had every intention of coming back to claim her, but everything changed. Brent Waterhouse signed me, and within three months, I had a record contract and a tour. I also had a life no one would envy if they truly knew how it was. They say hindsight is twenty/twenty. I'd been blinded by good intentions, and if I had it to do all over again, I'd do it differently. I looked back at Mandy before I exited and wished I could turn back the clock. I'd really screwed everything up.

The chill of the air and the shriek of a high-pitched voice hit me the minute I walked out the door. "Oh, my God, it's Beau Tinsel!" Theresa Platt ran at me like her brake lines had been cut. I'd recognize her anywhere—her breasts, anyway. She was top heavy, and I never understood how she didn't topple over. She had defied gravity for years.

Oomph, she plowed into me, knocking me back against the glass. The window shuddered, making everyone inside the Sweet Shop jump from their seats. At the counter, Mandy watched me, Greg's mouth was moving, but she was all eyes on me, and I liked that. I saw that look before; it was an ounce of jealousy mixed with a pound of curiosity. I could make that work.

Theresa's hands slid down my chest, gripping at the felt of my pea coat. "When did you get back?" she cooed.

"Last night. Listen, I've got a call I have to take. Can we catch up later?" I didn't want to catch up with her, but I wasn't one for being rude.

"Sure thing, sweets. I hear Mandy is back too, with a kid." The way she said "kid" like it was sour candy irritated me. I'd spent a bit of time with Tommy today while his mother ignored me. He was an awesome kid.

"His name is Tommy and he's amazing." The urge to defend the kid surprised me. I had never given kids much thought, but Tommy was Mandy's, and that made him special.

"I'm not much for little boys, but I like the big ones." She reached up and touched my hair. "I own the shop across the street. I could give you a trim."

I combed my hand through my hair. I bet she was willing to offer her services, but I was pretty certain it had nothing to do with her beauty shop or scissors.

"Sounds great, I'll catch you later." A quick glance over my shoulders showed Mandy was still looking. I hadn't liked that man's lips on her, but two could play that game. I pressed my lips to Theresa's cheek, and when I turned to wave goodbye to Mandy, her look had changed to a pound of jealousy and a ton of pissed off. I *really* liked that.

I just made it home when my cell phone rang. "Hey, Brent, what do you have for me?" I was in negotiations for a three-record contract. The advance would set me up for life.

"Can you be back the twenty-third to meet with Rocco?"

Any other day, I would have made the meeting happen, but the look I'd seen in Mandy's eyes told me she was angry enough to still care, which meant there was hope, and right now, I was here in Bell Mountain, and hope was all I could bank on.

"No can do. I've got some personal stuff to take care of. See if you can postpone it." I never shied away from making my demands. I'd been making decisions for myself since the day I left town. Some were good, and some were complete failures, but there was one decision

I had made that needed clearing up, and now that I was here, I couldn't leave Bell Mountain until that was done.

"You don't keep a producer like Rocco Piat waiting. Everyone is clamoring to work with him." Brent didn't like pushing a bigwig like Rocco to the side, but he worked for me, and he'd have to fight for what I wanted. He could slay all the work dragons while I slayed the ones at home.

"Figure it out." I cut the call before he could argue.

"Beau, is that you?" Mom called from the living room as if anyone else would be walking in the front door unannounced.

"Yep, it's me." Once in the living room, I tossed my coat on the corner chair and took a seat beside her. She was watching some true crime show. "Getting ideas on how to off your next husband?" It was an awful thing to say, but we both laughed. Sometimes, all you could do was laugh in the face of misfortune. "What's for dinner?"

"Oh, I'm taking Tommy for pizza with Annie. Mandy had some errands to run, and since I'm not getting any grandchildren from you, I have to steal Annie's."

"I take it I'm not invited?" I leaned into my mom and let her wrap her arm around my shoulder. It had been a long time since she had mothered me, and it felt good.

"You can come if you like awful pizza and animated stuffed animals." She pulled her fingers through my hair. I'd always loved when she did that. "Did you see Mandy today?"

"You know I did because you must have talked to Annie. I met Tommy. He's a great kid. Scared me for a moment. He looks just like me."

"Yes, he does. If I didn't know better, I'd have said he was yours as well, but of course, he isn't. His dad is some famous French chocolatier, and he wasn't interested in being a dad. It's too bad because Mandy would make an amazing wife."

Thinking about Mandy as someone else's wife stabbed at my heart. It was funny how I hadn't thought of her with anyone else until I saw her kissing Greg. Even when I thought she was married, her husband was faceless and nameless, but now Greg's lips on hers would be all I would see when I closed my eyes tonight.

"You know what Mom, I'm going to check on the cabin." It was my favorite thinking place, and I needed a plan. When I left Colorado, I wanted different terms with Mandy. I wasn't sure what those terms would be, but I didn't want my life to be void of her presence. I'd settle for whatever she'd offer at this point.

Mom's flat expression turned into a smile. "You always did your best thinking out there. Stay off the ice." I snuggled into her side for a minute longer before I left.

The drive to the cabin was short and scenic. I often saw a deer or two on the way, but today, the roads were empty. There wasn't a person or animal in sight, and the lack of everything was comforting. Sometimes, the answers to life's most pressing problems were found in the stillness.

Once inside the garage, I killed the SUV's engine

and sat for a time. The minute I walked into the cabin, I'd be inundated with memories from my past. The weekends Dad and I spent alone fishing. The nights Mandy and I spent naked in front of the fire. Those were some of the best times of my life. This was my happy place. It was a two-bedroom shack that sported the barest of essentials, and yet, it was the place where I'd felt the richest.

Climbing the two steps, the door creaked open and I flipped on the lights. Mom had kept the place clean. She'd threatened to update the cabin, to bring it into the twenty-first century, but I always fought her. To change it, would change what it meant to me.

Mandy loved this place, too. She always gave her mom a hard time for hanging on to things like her record player, and the television set with the rabbit ears, but Mandy wasn't much different. Mandy didn't let go of people or things that easily, and that gave me a glimmer of hope.

When Mom said, "so what if you find yourself in love with her again," I thought, *little do you know, but I've never fallen out of love with her*. The question was…could she ever love me again? In my gut, I yearned for that possibility. When I gave her up, I gave up any chance of ever being happy.

I turned out the lights. In the dark, I sat in front of the window and watched the sun set and the moon cast a glow over the lake. In the distance, the outline of a dark fishing hut sat in the center of the lake, abandoned for the night. Headlights came and went as cars passed

along the highway, but the tranquility of the lake hypno-
tized me.

Out of the shadows stepped a silhouette. Mandy's
blonde hair soaked in the moon's rays. Step by cautious
step, she walked to the end of the dock and sat with her
legs dangling over the edge. I wanted to get her alone
and the universe gifted me this opportunity. I wasn't
going to blow it. With a handful of chocolate kisses and
a blanket wrapped around my arm, I approached.

"You're trespassing, you know."

CHAPTER FIVE

MANDY

Peaceful serenity had settled over me until his voice broke the silence, scaring me near to death. I almost fell off the dock and onto the icy crust of the lake —the same lake where our fathers had died.

"Shit, Beau. What are you doing here?" My heart beat like a mixer on high.

"I should ask you the same. I'm here because I own the property. You?" He unfolded the blanket and wrapped it around my shoulders. Beau had always been sweet like that.

It would have been wise to stand and leave, but I couldn't bring myself to do it, so I wrapped the blanket around me like armor. Beau and I had some unfinished business, and maybe attacking it head-on would be the best way to bury it and move forward. When I left for New York, I wanted to be able to say Beau and I had come to terms with our past.

"I came here to think. To feel closer to my dad." My

voice softened to a murmur. "To figure out how to deal with you."

Beau sat beside me and pulled half the blanket over his shoulder. Sitting next to him took me back years to when we sat on this same dock that final summer night. He was leaving the next day to go to Los Angeles and we took advantage of every minute we had together.

"Have you figured it out yet?"

"No, because I just got here, and then you interrupted my train of thought."

"Would you like me to leave?"

My brain yelled "yes," but my heart screamed "no." Just being near him like this made me want him. I never got over him, but I needed to.

"No, we need to talk, but I'm not sure if I'm ready for it." *Get it out and over with. Treat it like a Band-Aid; rip it off fast so it's less painful.*

"Let's catch up first, and then we can talk about other things." He pulled a handful of chocolate kisses from his pocket and offered me one. Where was my peppermint when I needed it? Hadn't it always been the perfect mix for us? Weren't we once the perfect combination? Time changed everything.

Taking a silver-wrapped candy from his palm, I peeled back the foil. "Congratulations on your success." I tried to imbibe excitement into the words, but they fell flat. It was his success that had derailed our future.

"Thanks, it's been a journey, for sure." He lined the wrapped candies in a row. We hunched together under the blanket. When my knee touched his, we froze in place. For two people who used to know each other from the inside out, we were acting like strangers. But, that's exactly what we were—intimate strangers.

"I went to one of your concerts." Telling him was like divulging a dirty little secret.

"You did?" He shifted and our knees rubbed together. That little bit of contact sent my nerves skittering. "Which one? You should have contacted me, and I could have met you for coffee or something."

"I saw you in New York, but we weren't talking anymore."

The elephant in the room stomped across the dock and sat with us—its presence heavy enough to collapse the world around us. Yes, we had stopped talking. Well, Beau had stopped talking, and I had stopped trying to get him to change his mind.

"Do you like New York?" He moved the candy around, first making a line, then a triangle, and then a square.

"Not really, I have an ass for a boss, and it's hard to find good help to take care of Tommy." At the mention of Tommy, Beau smiled.

"Tommy's a great kid." Those damn sapphire eyes glinted under the moon at me. Their cool color always had the opposite effect on me. My body burned under his gaze. "Where's his dad?"

"In Paris." He didn't need the details. What was the point? Beau would be gone soon. We weren't best buddies anymore, but it would be nice to not feel so conflicted when it came to him.

"Explain?"

"There's nothing to explain, he was just another guy

who didn't see the value of staying with me." The hurt in my voice couldn't be masked. It shattered me to think of the people who'd tossed me aside.

Beau bit his lip. "It wasn't like that with us." He shifted again so he was facing me. The blanket had fallen from his shoulders and pooled on the dock. When I wrapped it around me, I clenched the soft fabric to my chest.

"It doesn't matter." I buried my face in the material, but Beau pulled it away.

"It matters to me. I created this gaping hole in our friendship, and it's up to me to fill it with something."

"How about the truth?" Damn stupid tears ran down my cheeks. "I think I deserve the truth, don't you?"

"Yes, I do."

"Was it someone else? I've seen you with everyone from starlets to models. I get it."

"No, it wasn't someone else. It was always you. It's still you." His fingers walked up the plaid blanket and settled on my knees.

Talk about head-spinning. Mine was about to take off from my shoulders. "That doesn't make sense."

"It's the truth."

"Tell your truth to Theresa Platt, but be careful. As the town hairdresser, she's known for her blow jobs and bangs."

"I love that you're jealous."

"I'm not jealous. You've been gone for years. I've moved on." The lie frayed my tattered heart.

"Yes, I saw that when you kissed that man today.

45

How'd you find a new beau so soon? Didn't you get here the day I did?"

I hated his use of the word beau. There was, and would only be, one Beau in my life, and he'd turned out to be a complete jerk. I threw the blanket off my shoulders and hopped to my feet. Anger was heating me from the inside out. "That was Greg Anderson, you idiot." My voice pitched and pulled as I towered over him.

Beau's face twisted in confusion. "Isn't he gay? I swear, I heard he was gay, but I saw him kiss you, and that was a bit too friendly for my taste."

"He's not into me or any other girl, but he had it in his head that you'd get jealous if he kissed me, so he did." Beau's emotions were always easy to read. Right then, he was awash in relief, and that made one little butterfly flutter in my stomach. Beau still cared, at least a smidge. "Greg's a friend."

"Tommy explained that to me. He said Greg was a boy, and a friend, and so he was your boyfriend." He reached up and touched my hand. His energy surged through me like it always had. Beau Tinsel was a drug I hadn't kicked. "Sit down, please." He tugged at my fingers until I folded and sat cross-legged in front of him.

"Do you remember when we used to sit like this and play chicken?" He had always won and my hands were beet red before we were done, but it just gave him a reason to kiss them, and somehow, that always turned into more.

"You want to play?" He held out his hands. His eyes widened to challenge me, and I could never pass up a challenge.

"You're on."

I laid my palms on top of his and before I knew it, he'd slapped the top of mine several times. He always had quick reflexes. I figured it came from all those years of playing guitar.

Time after time, he nailed my hands, slapping the tops until they turned red. Then, he missed one, giving me a shot at causing him a little sting. It was the least I owed him after he'd eviscerated me. With careful planning, I shot my hands out and tried to slap the tops of his, but as usual, I was too slow.

"You still suck at this." He dragged my hands to his mouth where he kissed the redness. It was like being transported back in time when life was simpler. Caught up in his lips moving across my knuckles, I leaned forward and so did he. And just like old times, his mouth covered mine, and I was eighteen and in love again.

He tasted of chocolate and desire. His tongue danced with mine to a beat I couldn't hear, but I felt all the way to my core. What had been a single butterfly a moment before turned into a kaleidoscope that churned from my stomach to my heart. Caught up in the moment, I relished the feel of him in my arms and the taste of him on my lips, but this wasn't right. This was like make-up sex. It was good in the moment, but the feelings never lasted long. Betrayal was hard to forget. Even the perfect kiss couldn't erase the deep wounds he'd caused.

I pulled away from him and looked into his lust-clouded eyes. I'd loved that look in the past, but today, I couldn't fall under his spell. "I can't do this. I'm not that girl anymore. I'm over you." The words sounded true, but they felt hollow as they slipped from my lips. I was far from over him.

"Your kiss says something different, Mandy. That kiss was long overdue."

"Something is long overdue, but it's not a kiss, it's an explanation."

He looked around the dock and groaned. "You're right. I owe you." He ran his hands through his mop of hair. "Do you want to come inside?"

Inside sounded nice, but after that kiss, I wasn't sure I'd be able to rein myself in a second time. I was weak when it came to Beau. I couldn't trust myself to not fall into his arms or his bed.

"No, here is fine, and then I have to go. Tommy will be waiting for me."

"Tommy is out with our mothers, who, by the way, lied to get us here."

"So, no twisted ankle for your mother?"

"No, did a mysterious accident befall yours, as well?"

"Yes, she fell and sprained her wrist." *But did she really?* I'd watched mom whip up pancakes this morning but couldn't remember which hand held the spoon. "Oh, my God, her whole story was a farce to get me home."

"Unbelievable." Beau shook his head.

"I believe their hearts are in the right place, but where was yours ten years ago?" And there was that elephant again, and he was lifting his trunk too high to ignore.

48

Beau reached out and grasped my hands. "I told you, it's always been you."

"Does that work for all the other girls?" Sarcasm dripped from every word.

"Mandy, there has never been another girl. Not in the way things were with you."

I'd seen at least twenty photos that would prove his statement wrong. "So, I wasn't the only one you screwed and forgot? I can't say it makes me feel any better to be in a large pool of recipients."

"It wasn't like that. Let me explain." He gripped my hands, refusing to let them go.

"Let's hear it so I can go."

"The last night we were at this cabin. You were ready to quit school and follow me to California."

"I would have followed you anywhere." That was the honest truth. If he'd said, "come with me Mandy," I would have happily quit school and followed him to California.

"That was the problem. I wanted you to chase your dream, too. I would have taken you with me in a second, but you needed to finish high school."

"You were right to leave me behind. I just don't understand the rest." The pain of the last conversation we'd had rushed forward and caught in my heart. "Six months later, you disappeared from my life."

"You need to understand that I was thinking of you."

His grip forced me to stay seated when all I wanted to do was run. "Were you thinking of me when you showed up at the music awards with Inga Knight?" The woman was dressed in lingerie and stilettos, hanging on his arm like a bad handbag.

"No, that was just business. A required promotional opportunity—for her." He moved his head so wherever I looked, I had to look at him. "I loved you enough to let you go."

I had enough. With a yank, I freed myself and fled. It only took him three steps to catch up to me and pull me back.

"Damn it, Mandy, You asked for an explanation and you're going to stay and listen to it." He pushed me against the timber railing. Behind me, the moon reflected off the icy lake, creating a glow that lit up the forest around us. "I loved you. More than you'd ever imagine, and letting you go felt like ripping out my innards."

"You ripped out my heart, Beau, and then you stomped on it by writing songs like 'Wrecked' and 'Hopeless.'"

"Those songs were what I was feeling. I wrote them as a way to cope with not having you."

Cuss words weren't my thing in general. Not because I was opposed to expletives, but because I'd had to tone down my language when I'd had a child, but this moment called for the granddaddy of foul words.

"You stupid asshole. You had to cope? You broke up with me." I beat against his chest, but he didn't budge. He stood there and took every strike.

"I didn't, I just walked away so you could chase your dream."

"What in the hell are you talking about? My dream was to be with you."

He sucked in a breath and pulled my hands to his heart. I could feel the pounding in his chest like it would burst at any second. "You called and told me you'd been accepted into culinary school. Not any school, but the most coveted in Paris, and you were going to give that up to be with me."

"God, Beau, don't you get it. I loved you. I would have given anything to be with you."

"That's why I had to let you go. You deserved more than a tour bus and a green room."

"Why didn't you tell me?" Tears streamed down my face.

"Because you wouldn't have listened. You would have jumped on the first bus to California, and I couldn't do that to you. Besides, life on the road sucked. The guys that had girlfriends rarely did when they returned. Jealousy ate at them until there was nothing left to salvage. I didn't want that to happen to us. I didn't want you to regret choosing me. I wanted you to fulfill your dreams and you would never have if you'd stayed with me."

His words were like a punch to the gut. He'd cut me loose so I could be something other than his girl? "That's bullshit and you know it."

He dropped to his knees in front of me. "I swear to you. I wanted what was best for you." His head sank against my thighs.

"And you were qualified to decide for me?" My voice

was savage in its delivery. "You let me go for my own good?"

"I did. I loved you. I still love you."

"You love me?" I screamed. "Where were you when I came home from Paris? Where have you been the last six and a half years?"

"You came back and had a son. You'd fallen in love and moved on. I didn't want to interfere."

Anger was a powerful force, and with it came unimaginable strength. With a fierce push, I sent Beau flying across the dock. "I'm so mad at you right now. I was never in love. I slept the guy because he reminded me of you, but he wasn't you." I stomped over to where Beau sat on the dock. "Or maybe he was exactly like you because the minute things got a bit complicated, he abandoned me, too."

"I didn't know."

"How could you? You'd disappeared, which is what I want from you right now. Get out of my life, Beau Tinsel. I don't want you, and I don't need you. You had no right to decide for me." It took me seconds to bolt from the dock and get to my car. The key slid into the ignition, and when I turned it, a clunk and a thunk were all I heard outside of Beau's call for me to stop.

CHAPTER SIX

BEAU

She pounded on the steering wheel with open palms. Despite her window being closed, I heard several colorful words spill from her mouth. Pissed off didn't begin to describe how she was feeling. I knew this girl, and even though I hadn't seen her in years, she was still the same Mandy I fell in love with as a kid.

I yanked on the door handle only to find it locked. Frustrated, I pounded on the window. I'd been so stupid. I'd done what I'd thought was right for her, and in the end, I'd messed up both of our lives.

"Mandy, open the door."

"No," she screamed.

"Come on, baby, unlock the door," I pleaded with no success. "At least pop the hood so I can look."

She turned her head, and when I saw her teary eyes, I was heartbroken. I did this to her. I hurt her again.

"Go away, and don't call me baby." Her pained voice brought tears to my eyes.

"I'm not leaving you. Open the damn door." I put

both hands on the window and pressed my nose to the cold glass. "Please, Mandy, let me help." She slumped against the seat and scrubbed her face with her palms.

"Haven't you done enough?"

"I've hurt you. I realize that, but at least let me get you home safe. Tommy will be coming home, and I know you'll want to be there." Using her son was unfair, but I had a feeling Mandy would soften when it came to her boy. The one thing I always knew about Mandy was she was an all-in kind of girl. That was part of the reason I forced her away. She would have never gone to Paris if she thought there was a chance to come to California with me. I never wanted her to regret that decision, so I made a different one for her. Little did I know, things would turn out the way they did. I expected her to come home from culinary school and then we could figure it out, but she came home with a son and moved to New York. She'd moved on, or so I thought. I was an idiot.

She unlocked the door and climbed out of the Jeep. "Take me home, please." She gave me a hard stare. "Where's your car?" With her hands shoved in her coat pockets, she walked to the back tire and kicked it. "Damn car." Then, she hopped on one foot and cussed to herself.

"Don't hurt yourself."

"Kicking the tire just saved you from the end of my boot."

"Fair enough." I stood in front of her and grasped her shoulders. "Kick my ass, punch my face, I deserve it."

"You do, but all I want to do is go home. Take me home."

"Car's in the garage." I settled my hand on her back and guided her to the back of the cabin.

"You never parked in the garage before."

"People change."

She came to a dead stop and turned to look at me. "They sure do." I didn't like the way she said that. Sure, I'd changed, but I was still the guy she fell in love with years ago. I'd made a stupid mistake that I had every intention of rectifying. I wasn't going anywhere until Mandy Sawyer was back in my life, back in my arms, and back in my bed. One look at her in the Sweet Shop and she was already back in my heart. I never stopped loving her.

Once I got her in the car, I took the scenic route home, driving past our old haunts, hoping to soften her resolve to push me away. She was oblivious to our journey while she made arrangements to have her car towed. Once she hung up, she realized we were on Diamond Lane. She sat up and craned her neck to see the old Grady house. At least something made her take notice. I pulled over, turned off the engine, and stepped out of the car.

It took her a few minutes to follow, but I knew she would. She was a sucker for the old house. Sadly, it was dilapidated and falling apart. It had been vacant for years. In disrepair, no one had the money, time, or inclination to fix it. The white siding was now gray, and the wrap-around porch sagged in so many places, it looked like the track of a roller coaster.

"It's so sad that no one ever bought the place. It would have been perfect for a family." She ran her fingers over the trim of the broken-down gate.

"It needs to be leveled and rebuilt."

She gasped. "What's wrong with you? This house is a piece of history. It needs to be restored."

"Do you have any idea how much it would cost to restore this place? A brand new house could be built on the land for half the price of restoration."

"How can you claim to be forward-thinking with my life, and so shortsighted with this house?" She unlatched the gate and walked through the ankle-high snow. "Preserving the past is important."

She looked beautiful standing in front of the old house. She belonged there. I could see her rocking our baby on the porch swing, but I was getting ahead of myself. How would I get her to love me again if she didn't trust me or want to talk to me?

"Preserving the past *is* important. We have a past that needs preservation as well. Would you be willing to put as much time and energy into resurrecting us as you would this old house?"

"It's not the same and you know it." She gave one last look at the house and walked back to the car.

I raced ahead to open her door. "No, it's not the same. Old houses aren't people."

"Bingo, and although you can repair a roof, it's so much more difficult to repair a broken heart. Impossible, maybe." She slid into the front seat and pulled the door shut, leaving me isolated and alone. Was she telling me the tear in her heart was irreparable? I would disagree, and I intended to prove her wrong.

She sat tall in her seat, looking forward as if we were strangers, and in many ways, we were. However, we had a lot of history, and I couldn't imagine either of us had changed that much. "Give me a chance to be your friend again." I knew being her friend would never be enough, but it was a start.

She shifted and looked at me. Even in the dark, her eyes glistened by the moonlight. The green depths said more than she probably wanted to share. "In less than two weeks, I'll be back in New York and you'll be," she spread her palms out in question, "wherever you are."

"Then, we have limited time to make this work." When I reached over to pat her hand, she pulled it to her chest as if it would shield her from me. Nope, I would be relentless until Mandy decided I was once again worth her time.

Tommy and our mothers were pulling into the driveway when we arrived. He exited the car with boundless energy. Racing toward us, I expected him to bypass me and fly straight into his mother's arms, but he didn't.

"Beau," he yelled. I lifted him into my arms and swung him around. "Hey sport, how was pizza?" Mandy stood to the side and watched. She smiled from her lips to her eyes at Tommy. When her eyes settled on me, she crimped her mouth tight.

Tommy turned my head with his little gloved hands so that I was looking at him. "I got a water pistol with the tickets I won from the games I played. Then, we went to the crap store and got glitter."

"Craft, Tommy, it's called a craft store." Mandy tried to maintain a stern expression, but I could see the smile twitching at the corner of her mouth.

My eyes locked with hers. "In all fairness, both are right. It depends on your perspective." I set Tommy on his feet and grabbed hold of his hand. "What are you going to do with the glitter besides make a mess?" In the distance, both moms watched the scene unfold.

"We're making ornaments with wishes. Do you have any wishes, Beau?" His baby blue eyes searched my face for an answer. Tommy was young, but he was an old soul. His expressive eyes and his inquisitive approach to life pulled me deeper into his charms.

I made sure to look at Mandy before I answered. "I have a lot of wishes, Tommy." I hoped she would see the truth in my eyes.

"Grandma Sarah and Grandma Annie said that we could have cookies and milk while we made our," he pulled me down and whispered, "crap," into my ear.

Laughter too robust to control burst from my lips. "Is that right? The *Grandma's* said that?" I looked toward the car, expecting to see them, but they had already escaped into the house. "I wouldn't miss cookies and milk for the world. Let's go." Hand in hand, we walked toward the door.

Pulling up the rear, Mandy spoke. "Tommy, I'm sure Mr. Tinsel is busy and has things to do."

"No, Mommy, he just said he has wishes. It would be *crinimal* to waste his wishes." And there were those puppy dog eyes again. I watched the play between mother and son, and I fell more in love with both right then.

"It's criminal, Tommy, the *M* comes first." She folded her hand over his and we walked into the house together.

Tommy gave us the slip and bolted to the kitchen, leaving Mandy and me in the entry. "Don't encourage him. He's desperate for a man's attention, but you're leaving, and so are we. I don't want to see him hurt."

"That's not my intention. He's a great kid, and I like him a lot."

I followed her gaze toward the kitchen. "I like him too, and that's why you need to stay away from him. You'll only exit his life and wound his little soul. He's too young for that."

"Give me a break." I pressed my hands to her shoulders and backed her up to the wall. "I was nineteen and thought I was making the right choice. I admit I was wrong."

"Tell that to someone who cares." Her quivering voice belied her intended I-don't-give-a-shit attitude.

"I remember a time when these lips were made for kissing." I pinned her in place with my hips while I ran my thumb over her lush lips. "When did you become such a cynic?"

"About ten years ago when you disappeared with my heart." She squirmed to free herself. The friction of her hips caused a painful strain in my jeans, but I wouldn't let her go. I couldn't let her walk away without letting her feel how much she affected me. She gave a frustrated growl as she pushed at my chest. When I covered her mouth with mine, she was silenced. No one existed in that moment but us. Our bodies pressed together while she allowed me to explore her mouth with eagerness. What was once an uncomfortable tug at my jeans now became an unbearable ache. My zipper felt like a guillotine threatening to sever my head. I needed her in the worst and best of ways. No…being Mandy's friend would never be enough.

CHAPTER SEVEN

MANDY

Tommy raced around the corner and plowed into us. "Mommy, it's time to…" His eyes opened wide. "You were kissing. K-I-S-S-I-N-G, Mommy and Beau were kissing in a tree," he sang.

"Come here, squirt." Beau picked Tommy up and threw him over his shoulder. "If you stop trying to embarrass your mom, I'll teach you a new song during the week. I'll even show you how to play the guitar."

"A real guitar?"

"Yes, my guitar." He flipped Tommy over and landed him on his feet. With a gentle coaxing, Beau turned him toward the kitchen. "Tell the Grandmas we'll be right there."

The fight drained out of me as I watched the two of them together. Beau was so right for Tommy and so wrong for me. I needed steadfast and stable. Beau was a nomad. He traveled the world and tasted its wares. That was great for a single guy with hundreds of groupies, but

I needed a family man and Beau had already proved he didn't have the staying power. *But that kiss…*

"We were interrupted." He leaned into me and nuzzled my neck. White, hot passion raged through my body and settled in my core. My knees buckled from the heated breath that caressed my skin. If it weren't for the hands he'd placed on my hips, I would have puddled on the floor. "I plan to finish what we started." He pressed his mouth to mine and pulled my lower lip between his. With a gentle suckle, he pulled away with a pop. "Tommy's waiting. We have wishes to make." He stepped back and devoured me with his eyes. There was no doubt what he'd wish for, the lust had turned his sapphire eyes to indigo. I needed distance. I needed perspective. I needed to stop this madness with Beau.

With my shoulders pulled back, I sucked in enough courage for a bold-faced lie. "There's nothing to finish. The kiss was nice, but nothing to tweet about."

"That's a shame." He cradled my cheek in the warm palm of his hand like he used to when he loved me. "And I thought you were enjoying it. Time to up my game." He flashed a white smile and left me by the front door. What was I going to do about Beau?

It took ten minutes to steady my heart rate, and another five, along with a splash of water, to dull the red that flushed my cheeks.

When I entered the kitchen, everyone was asses to elbows in glue and glitter. Tommy sat at the table, hovering over his tiny piece of paper. His arms folded around it like a fortress. Beau was dipping his pine cone tips in glue and our mothers were dumping more glitter onto the paper plates.

Sarah Tinsel pulled me into her arms. "It's so good to see you, sweetheart." She hugged me close for longer than needed and before she relinquished her grip on me, she said, "he's a good man, Mandy, he just needs a good woman to guide him." She pushed back and kissed my cheek. Expressive eyes ran in the Tinsel family. Sarah's were filled with optimism.

"Your turn, Mandy." Mom handed me a pine cone and a slip of paper.

"No thanks, I'm fresh out of wishes." I set the materials back on the table and walked to the refrigerator. "Is anyone hungry?"

Beau lifted his glittered hand. "Starved," he said. His tone was full and sexy, and I wasn't positive he was talking about filling his stomach.

"Omelet?"

"I'd love to taste whatever you have to offer." It was obvious why he sold millions of records. His voice alone could melt the pants off a frigid woman, but when you stirred that with sexual innuendo, no girl was safe.

"Don't get your hopes up. It's only a cheese omelet." Not wanting him to see the heat in my cheeks, I stuck my head in the cold refrigerator and rooted around for ingredients.

Twenty minutes later, Beau and I were scrunched at the end of the Formica table eating.

"Amazing," he said. "You never cooked like this when we were kids."

"I didn't have years of technique pounded into me

back then." I lifted my fork and watched the melted cheese string down to the plate. With a swirl, I severed the strands.

"Pounded into you sounds intriguing," he whispered.

A glance around the kitchen showed that no one was paying attention to our conversation. Mom and Sarah were mooning over Tommy and the way he was applying glitter to his pine cone. "This one's for Mommy," I heard him say. "She can fill it with her wish."

I let out a sigh of defeat. "Mom, hand me a scrap of paper so I can make my wish." Mom rushed to the table with a pen, and the paper, and a huge smile. Somehow, she'd won—again.

When her hand crossed in front of my face, I noticed globs of glitter stuck to her bandage. With a shake of my head, I pulled her wrist in front of me. "Don't you think it's time you let go of this farce? I know, and you know, that you didn't fall. You didn't sprain anything, and you certainly don't need to perpetuate the lie."

She tried to pull her hand away, but I had a six-year-old, and I was trained in evasion tactics. "Stop fussing, Mom." I released the clips and began to unwind the long cloth bandage.

"Mandy, you're hurting me."

Tired of being manipulated by everyone around me, I wasn't swayed at her feeble attempts to extend the ruse. Enough was enough. Mom flinched as I tore at what remained of the bandage.

My throat tightened and my stomach twisted when I

saw her injury. Mom's wrist was the color of an eggplant. She had told the truth. She had fallen, and I hadn't believed her. "Oh. God. Mom. I'm so sorry." I cradled her hand in mine and ran my thumb across the bruise. It was angry and inflamed, and real.

Beau stepped into action by sitting my mom in his chair and gathering a baggy of ice. He wrapped the pack in a towel and set it on her wound.

"Thank you, Beau." Her voice was sweet and gentle and showed her sense of appreciation. When her eyes turned to me, they held something completely different. Gone was the love and softness and in its place was plain old hurt.

"Mandy, when did you become such a cynic." Those were almost the same words Beau had thrown at me earlier. Where had I gone wrong? I had allowed life's bumps to throw me off track, to change me, and I needed to get myself straight.

Tears threatened to spill from my eyes. "I'm so sorry." Words were not enough to make amends for doubting her. She'd never doubted me. She hadn't been easy on me, but not once in my entire life had she not been there for me. I was the worst daughter.

"Oh, honey, it's all right. I can't say I wouldn't have resorted to a fib to get you home." She smiled in Sarah's direction. Turning back, her eyes landed on Beau. "Don't be angry at your mom either, she was inspired by my mishap."

"I'm not angry. I'm grateful."

He stared at me like he was looking into my soul, searching for anything that said I felt the same.

Without thought, I reached across and squeezed his hand.

Mom broke the moment when she dropped a grenade on the conversation. "Oh, before I forget. We have an order for three hundred Christmas wreath cookies tomorrow. They want green icing and a red bow."

"What?" My shock settled around us like a thick fog. "I can't make three hundred cookies along with everything else with only Misty to help."

"Really, Mandy? Is this how the whole trip is going to be—you finding fault with everything? What happened to my can-do girl? Don't worry, I've got a temp for you."

I hung my head, hoping she wouldn't see my real feelings. What was a temp supposed to do if I had to spend hours training them? I'd been home a day, and I was already bone-deep tired, but I forced a smile and lifted my head. "Sounds super."

"Where is your car?" Mom cocked her head toward the front door like x-ray vision would allow her to see it.

"It wouldn't start, so I had it towed. I'll have to borrow your car tomorrow."

Mom lifted her shoulders with indifference. "That's no problem. Sarah and I are taking Tommy to see Santa."

"If you don't stop spoiling him, he won't want to go back to New York."

"Oh, no…you've discovered my evil plan." She cackled like a witch. "You look exhausted, Mandy, Sarah and I will take care of Tommy, why don't you go to bed. It's going to be a busy day tomorrow."

The groan slipped out on its own. I tried to cover it with an exaggerated yawn, but no one was buying it. "Let me make my wish and then I'm out of here." I looked around the room and thought about what I'd wish for. There was only one logical thing to hope for, so I jotted it down and shoved it into the pine cone Tommy had decorated for me.

After kissing him goodnight, I hugged the mothers and nodded toward Beau who was back to decorating pine cones. Then, I trudged upstairs. Walking into my old room was like opening a time capsule. Why I kept the pink canopy bed all these years was beyond me, and yet it wasn't. I accused Mom of holding on to the past, but the truth was, I kept this bed because my father had built it, and I didn't have the heart to see it disappear. I always believed I'd have a little girl, and she'd sleep in the bed that her grandfather had built.

Tommy wouldn't even sit on it. I showed him my room when we'd arrived yesterday. He took one look at the pink lace that hung from the canopy and shook his head. He avoided it like it would suck the emerging manliness out of his body.

He did like the spider web in the corner though and cried when I said I was removing it. He made me trap its leggy occupant in a cup and relocate it outside before he would go to bed. Then, he climbed into the bed in the room next to mine and slept like the dead while I replayed every moment of the last ten years of my life. What I felt most was a gut-wrenching loss.

A knock at the door broke me from my musings. It didn't surprise me when Beau walked in and sat beside me on my bed. It felt comfortable. How many times had we sat here and done homework? Talked? Made out?

"Are you okay?" His sweetness was my undoing.

"Yes. No. Hell, I don't know." I threw my hands in the air. "It's all too much. Coming home. Seeing you. Working at the Sweet Shop. The kiss I wanted to hate but loved." *Shit, did I actually say that?*

"I loved it, too." His fingers ran through my hair, gripping me tight at the neck. "I want to love it more."

Every hormone in my body was screaming yes, but my mouth said, "No." I moved his hands from me and pressed them to those damn blue jeans that hugged his thighs in the most perfect way. "It's too much."

Beau nodded. "You're overthinking it, Mandy. Just go with it."

"I can't. Don't you understand, I have more to think about than me?" I rubbed my face with my palms.

"I'm not asking to kiss Tommy."

"You haven't asked to kiss me. You've just taken what you wanted. Don't I have a choice?"

His head snapped back like I'd slapped him. "Okay, no more unwelcome kisses." His voice sank with each word. He glanced around as if looking for an escape. With a pat on his legs, he rose. "I just wanted to make sure you were okay." He rocked back and forth on his heels and shoved his hands in his pockets. I'd rocked his confidence. What kind of terrible person was I becoming?

"Beau, it's not that I don't love your kisses. I do. It's

that I can't handle your kisses. I don't know how to navigate this mess." I hadn't been this truthful to anyone, including myself, in a long time.

"Mandy, I'd insist on navigating for both of us, but then you'd accuse me of taking away your choices. I've learned my lesson. I want your kisses, but I won't demand them. I'll wait until you're begging me for them. Until then, I'll prove that I'm a man you can trust. It's the least I can do for our friendship." He leaned forward like he was going to kiss me, but instead, he brought his lips a whisper away from my ear. "You will beg, Mandy. That's a promise I can make and keep."

CHAPTER EIGHT

BEAU

I wished I could have captured the look on Mandy's face before I left last night, or the look that must have been on my face when Mom and Annie told me I was the temp for the Sweet Shop.

Leaning against the rental car, I crossed my arms and waited for her to step out of the house. I didn't think the temperature could drop any further, but it was arctic cold, the kind you feel in your marrow. The smart thing would have been to wait in the warm car, but I knew Mandy, and she was on the stubborn side. Just to spite me, she'd walk by, pretending I wasn't taking up the entire driveway.

The rattle of the door handle sent my heart racing. I had less than two weeks to change Mandy's mind about me. The problem was, I didn't know what her mind was telling her. One minute, she appeared to like me, and the next, she appeared to loathe me.

When she turned around, she came to an abrupt

stop. "What are you doing here?" She pulled the collar of her jacket tight around her neck.

"I'm your temp for the day." I gave her an ain't-that-grand look and opened the door to the passenger side of the car for her.

"No way. I'm going to kill her." She shoved her hand into her pocket, rooting around for something. "Oh, my God, she took her keys back." She marched to the front door and tugged at the handle. "She locked me out."

"Well, I'm your driver, and I'm freezing, so if you could hurry up and get in the car, the parts of my body that haven't suffered from frostbite would be grateful." I pulled my gloved fingers to my mouth and huffed on them. The heat of my breath was eaten up by cold air that disappeared like a puff of smoke.

"Holy shit, Beau, what in the hell are you doing out here? What if you got frostbite and couldn't play your guitar?" She rushed toward me and pulled off my gloves, then began rubbing my fingers between her palms. She pulled them to her mouth and blew her peppermint breath across my knuckles. I never craved a candy kiss so bad in my life. I was chocolate, she was peppermint—we were perfect together.

I didn't want to pull my hand from in front of her mouth, but if we stood out front much longer, we would be permanent fixtures until the spring thaw. "In you go, but if you insist on putting your lips on me again, I have some preferred locations." I shot her a lecherous smile.

"I bet you do." She climbed into the car, and I rushed around to the driver's side to enter. With the heat pumped to high, we both held our fingertips against the vents. "I don't remember it being this cold."

"It's not normally this frigid, but Mom said something about an arctic shift. We're supposed to get a thaw just before Christmas." I put the car in reverse and pulled out of her driveway. This felt like old times when I'd driven her to school. Only then, I had a truck, and she usually slid across the bench and snuggled into my side. Back then, I didn't rush to put the heat on. I relished the feel of her body next to mine. I never thought I'd say it, but I missed that truck. The console that now sat between us felt like a continent.

"What is it you're supposed to help me with today? You're a musician, not a baker."

"How hard can it be? It's cookies for goodness sake."

"Did you just dis my occupation?" She spun in her seat as far as the belt would allow.

The heat of her temper warmed up the car by several degrees. Immediate backtracking and sucking up was needed. "I'm just saying that with your excellent tutelage, my sorry ass can help with something, even if it's dishes or running the cash register. Music is lyrical math, I'm pretty sure I can count back change."

She tucked a strand of blonde hair back into her knit cap. "That's a pretty big step down for a man who makes a gazillion dollars a concert." She picked up my thermal coffee cup. "Do you mind? I didn't have time to make a cup."

"Knock yourself out."

Out of the corner of my eye, I saw her pull the cup to her lips and drink long and slow. Just having something of mine close to her lips was great, but when she hummed with satisfaction, I smiled. I remember a time when she'd been beneath me and made that same sound.

"How do you always get the perfect mix?" A droplet rested on her lower lip. I wanted to pull the car over and lick it, but I settled for the sight of her pink tongue sliding from her mouth to sweep the drop away. Shifting in my seat, I was back to yesterday with a zipper threatening to make me a eunuch.

"It's all about the cow. You know…a half a cow and teaspoon of sugar." Wasn't that what she asked me just yesterday? *Had it been only a day?*

"You're such a smart ass."

"Yes, but I'm working harder on the smart than the ass. Give me a chance, Mandy." I pulled the SUV in front of the Sweet Shop. The inside lights were on, meaning someone was already hard at work. I exited and rushed to open Mandy's door. Her eyes held warmth; her lips stretched to a thin line. She was conflicted.

"We've got a lot to do." She marched toward the side door, leaving me behind. I rushed to get the door for her. I might have been stupid, I might have been an ass, but I was definitely a gentleman. My mom demanded it.

Misty was at the mixer, throwing sugar and butter into the big silver bowl. Her eyes rose to meet ours, and when she saw me standing behind Mandy, her jaw dropped along with the bag of sugar. White granules cascaded over the floor. Who knew a ten-pound bag of sugar could coat so many square feet?

Mandy looked at the mess on the floor and then at me. "That's your first job, Mr. Temp."

Misty's brows lifted. "Temp?" She pulled another bag of sugar from the shelf and emptied it into the mixing bowl. "This should be interesting."

"It's going to be something." Mandy's voice held a hint of amusement.

Misty was never a good whisperer, and I was grateful for her full-bodied voice. "Are you guys a thing again?" She leaned into Mandy. They stood at a distance from the mixer while I swept up the spill.

"No." Mandy's face pinched like she'd tasted something bitter. She hung up her coat, pulled an apron from the corner hook, and tossed a spare one to me. "Put this on to save your clothes."

My hand flew up to catch the white cloth. This was Mandy's world, and although initially shocked that I'd been catapulted into it, I was grateful to be here. I'd wheedle my way back into her life, one task at a time.

By mid-morning, I graduated from cleaner to cash register. At the rear counter, Misty and Mandy decorated hundreds of cookies. Word got out I was at the shop and the place was hopping with mostly women. I had no idea how difficult it was to pick out a muffin or a cookie, but the women in this town pondered over their selections for an interminable amount of time. This wasn't rocket science; it all came down to choice. By the fiftieth customer, I had it figured out. I tried my new approach when Theresa bounced in through the door.

"Hey, Beau." She tugged her already low-cut shirt lower. "I heard you were here." She glanced past me to Mandy. "If you needed something to keep you busy, I could have come up with something far more titillating." It surprised me to learn Theresa knew the word "titillating" and could pronounce it, but what surprised me most was the growl that came from Mandy. I loved that she was jealous.

"Hey, Theresa, it's good to see you again. You look lovely. Can I recommend a blueberry muffin? They aren't as sweet as you, but I think you'll enjoy one." I was playing with fire, but I liked it when Mandy was hot, if even only under the collar.

Theresa fluffed her bottle-blonde hair and grinned. "Oh, Beau baby, I'll take anything you want to give me."

When the empty tray hit the floor, all eyes turned toward Mandy. Her thin-lipped smile couldn't hide her annoyance. Her green eyes flashed with possessiveness. She wiped her hands on her apron, picked up the tray, and stalked toward the register.

"You've got stuff to finish in the back." She used her hip to slide me over. "Start with this." She pushed the empty tray into my hands. Theresa frowned and Mandy's smile conveyed sweet victory.

Little did she know, the victory had been mine.

In the back doing dishes, I heard the squeal of a very excited young man. "Mommy." When I turned around, Mandy was hugging Tommy tight to her chest. I dried my hands and walked to the door to look at mother and son. Although Tommy's dark hair and honeyed skin were in stark contrast to Mandy's light hair and fair complexion, one thing they shared was a heart-stopping smile. Tommy effervesced with happiness and joy, and so did his mom when she saw him. She used to gift me with that same smile when we were young. I wanted that back.

My mom and Annie were shooing everyone but Misty into the back room where I stood blocking the doorway.

"Good afternoon, Beau," Annie leaned in and kissed me on the cheek. "Your mom and I are taking over the afternoon shift. Lola will be in at three to close." I had no idea who Lola was and from Mandy's expression, neither did she.

"Lola?" Mandy walked over to the schedule. Her finger tapped down the row at each name. There were six in all. A look of irritation flashed across her face. "When did you hire all of these employees?" It was obvious Mandy was wondering why I needed to be here in the first place if there were others who could have filled in. I had to love our meddling mothers. They were providing an opportunity I would not have otherwise been given.

"They're kids, Mandy, they don't need much skill to clean and run the cash register."

I held up my hand. "I can vouch for that." Mandy twisted her lips from side to side. I wanted to grab a hold of her and soften the tension in them. One kiss and she'd be like a ragdoll in my arms, but I promised she'd beg, and I intended to keep that promise.

"We've got this, Mom. In fact, the big order is finished and the stock for the day is complete. I can handle the rest. You, Sarah, Beau, and Tommy don't have to be here."

"Nonsense. Sarah and I like to flirt with the old duffers. It's our afternoon thing. Would you deny us that pleasure? Besides, I promised Tommy you and Beau would hang the Christmas lights today. It's a toasty thirty degrees out so you better get moving before the sun goes down and takes what little warmth we have left in the day." Annie walked to the register and opened the overflowing cash drawer. "Wow, big sales day?"

Mandy looked at me, then back to her mom. "They didn't come in for the cookies, they just bought them as a courtesy."

"Beau, you might be my secret weapon. You're on tomorrow, by the way. Hathaway's wants their normal holiday order of one hundred chocolate-dipped candy canes, seven pounds of assorted fudge, and six dozen assorted cookies." With a flip of her uninjured wrist, we were dismissed.

"Stop meddling, Mom." Mandy removed her apron and tossed it on the stainless steel prep table. She looked at a smiling Misty and shook her head. "You too. You all need to stop." She walked to the counter and loaded several cookies into a bag. One glance at me and she pulled two chocolate-coated candy canes from the jar. "Let's go, we have lights to hang."

I swooped Tommy into my arms. He was big enough to hold his own, but I liked the feel of him sitting on my hip. I liked the smell of his shampoo, and the touch of his sticky fingers when they pulled at my scruff. Yep, I liked this kid.

"Have you eaten, champ?" It was past noon and I was starved. "How about a pit stop for fried chicken and waffles?" I loved Grady's Diner. Old Lou ran it like a drill sergeant. She told you what you were going to have and how you would feel about it. I hoped she was still there. She seemed ancient ten years ago.

"Can I just have waffles?" Tommy asked.

"Are you guys coming, or are you going to discuss lunch all day? I'm starving." Mandy stood outside of the SUV with her hands perched on her hips. Hips I'd felt last night. Hips I craved to grasp again, only next time, it would be while I was pounding some sense into her one thrust at a time.

After setting Tommy down, we rushed to the car to let her in. "Does your mom still get grumpy when she's hungry?"

"She's a poopy face when she's hungry."

Mandy gasped. "Tommy, that's not nice."

He climbed in the backseat and buckled up. "I'm sorry, Mommy, but it's true."

"You two are ganging up on me, and I don't think I like it." There wasn't an ounce of annoyance in her voice.

I shut their doors and rushed around to the driver's side. "If you feel you're being picked on, I can make it up to you. I used to have a way of making you feel better." My response was loaded with innuendo.

She growled like a bear and turned in her seat to face Tommy. "I'm as hungry as a bear, and I see a delicious boy that I could devour." She reached back and tickled him.

"Don't eat me. Eat Beau instead." My eyes opened wide. *Out of the mouths of babes.*

"Thanks a lot, Tommy." I glanced at his giggly expression in the rearview mirror. "I'm willing to take one for the team, Mandy. If you have to eat someone, I volunteer." Out of the corner of my eye, I watched her cheeks bloom red.

CHAPTER NINE

MANDY

"I heard you two were back." Old Lou wrapped the three of us in her withered arms. Tommy was smashed in the center of our human cookie. "Took you long enough to come see old Lou." She shuffled us to a corner booth and slapped three menus on the table, then shook her head and picked them back up.

"It's good to see you, Lou." I looked up at the old woman who had known us since we were born.

"My eyes aren't what they used to be, but you two still look good together, and that boy of yours is the spitting image of his daddy."

Tommy smiled, Beau laughed, and I sat quiet and stunned. Lou thought we were a family, and that couldn't have been further from the truth.

"He's a good looking boy, isn't he?" Beau reached over and patted Tommy's hand. He had been so open and welcoming to Tommy, seeing them together made me wish things were different.

"Damn straight. He's going to be a looker, just like

you were. You broke the heart of every girl in Bell Mountain." Lou turned her eyes to me. "You were the most envied girl in town. When did you guys get married?"

"Oh no, we aren't married," I blurted, and then fidgeted with the silverware to hide my discomfort. "We're not—"

"Kids nowadays." Lou popped Beau and me on the head with the stack of menus. Tommy was spared. "It's like you think marriage is old-fashioned. Love never goes out of style. Just look at Rusty and me, we're going on fifty years. That's fifty years that he's had to buy me an anniversary gift. You're missing out there. You should reconsider."

"It's not—"

"They kiss a lot," Tommy piped in, not willing to be overlooked.

"We do not." I covered his mouth with my palm. "He has no idea what he's talking about."

"Kissing is a good thing. It shows that the love is still there." She grabbed her order pad from her pocket and her pen from her ear. She pointed at Beau and me. "Chicken and waffles for you two and Lou's famous ginger beer." I always knew she gave us the ginger ale to ward off indigestion that the chicken and waffles were bound to cause. She pointed the tip of her pen toward Tommy. "You, young man, can tell Grandma Lou what you want, and I'll get it for you."

His little smile stretched from ear to ear. "I have another grandma," he said with excitement. What Tommy didn't understand was no one was a stranger in a small town, and often, they became like family. "Waffles please, Grandma Lou." Yep, he was a flirt. I sat and watched gruff old Lou Armstrong melt under my son's smile.

"You want to help Grandpa Rusty in the kitchen?" Lou held out her hand and Tommy readily took it.

"Tommy, don't touch anything and stay out of the way."

Beau reached his hands across the table and took mine. "She isn't going to let anything happen to him. Do you remember sitting on the prep table in the back listening to Rusty's fishing stories?"

The memory made me smile. "Yeah, do you really think he caught a forty-inch trout?" He was such a story spinner, and I never doubted him until this moment.

"Nope, but I believed it then, and each time I went fishing, I set that as the ultimate goal. A lot of fish got caught and released from my line. They failed to meet the minimum standard set by old Rusty."

My hands felt good in Beau's. His thumbs caressed my knuckles, and I knew I should have pulled them back. There was no use revisiting the past. In less than two weeks, we'd both be gone.

Lou slammed the ginger beer on the table. The amber liquid sloshed over the sides, but neither one of us broke our hold. "Tommy is making your meals. It will be a while." She looked at our clasped hands and grinned.

Beau's eyes were deep-ocean blue. Not a ripple of concern marred his tranquil expression.

"Why didn't you correct her when she assumed

Tommy was yours?" Some people chewed their lips when they were uncomfortable or nervous. Not me, I went all out and chewed the inside of my cheek. Depending on the tension I felt, I could chew a hole right through my skin. Today was one of those days where I might gnaw myself through and through.

Beau let go of my hands and picked up his drink. He sat in what appeared to be careful contemplation before he answered. "There was no harm in not correcting her. Besides, did you see Tommy's face light up? I wouldn't have extinguished that for anything."

"But he's not your son." My stomach was already getting acidy and upset. I picked up my drink and sipped at the fragrant brew. They say a smell can trigger a memory, but so can a taste. The last time Beau and I were here was my birthday. It was late May, and he was packed and ready to go. He'd slid a box across the table that held a locket with both our pictures. "Never take it off," he said, and the only time I removed it was the day Tommy was born. From that day forward, it sat in my jewelry box untouched and alone.

"No, he's not my son...yet." Beau's declaration caught me off guard.

"Not ever," I replied with a little more backbone than I was feeling. It's not that I wouldn't love a man like Beau to be Tommy's father; it was that Beau Tinsel had other priorities, and my son came first.

"Never say never, Mandy. I wasn't lying when I told Tommy that I'd be proud to call him son."

What was I supposed to say to that? Beau's track record had not been stellar when it came to me. He was a songwriter, a singer, and that made the words flow from his lips like sweet honey. He was trained to say what people wanted to hear.

I twisted my head, trying to ease the kink that had settled into my neck. "He's not a pawn in a game, Beau. He's a real live boy."

"You make him sound like Pinocchio. Of course, he's a real live boy, but it doesn't take DNA to make him mine. He was already mine the minute I laid eyes on him. So were you. Fight it all you want, Mandy. I screwed this all up a long time ago, and if it takes me ten years to fix it, so be it."

Tommy approached, wearing Rusty's cook jacket. They had put a piece of masking tape on top of the name and written "Tommy" with "Sous Chef" underneath. Lou brought up the rear with her arms covered in plates.

"Rusty says to keep that kid out of his kitchen. He's afraid of losing his job." Lou set the plates on the table and left.

Tommy slid into the booth next to me and pulled a five-dollar bill from his pocket. "Look what I earned. Now I have money to buy you a Christmas present." He waved the bill around like it was a hundred. To Tommy, it probably felt like he was rich.

"Wow," I said, trying to snatch the bill from his fisted palm. "We might have enough to retire soon."

We all dug into our food until Beau broke the silence. "Just like I remembered, crisp and greasy." He poured hot syrup all over his waffles and chicken. "So, you want Christmas lights?"

Tommy wiped his mouth with the back of his hand. "Yes, Grandma has these lights with big balls in all colors. Can we hang those?"

I knew the lights; they had to be as old as the percolator. "Tommy, those are really old. We'll try to hang them, but they may not work."

"Nonsense," Tommy said. That word was straight from my mother's mouth. "We already untangled them and tested them out after we hung the wish ornaments. I got to change out the bulbs that didn't light up."

Beau wiped his mouth with the back of his hand and smirked. "I think you and I should hang the lights. Maybe we can persuade your mom to make us some hot chocolate. What do you think?"

Tommy looked at Beau and me. He took a big drink of his milk. Before he could wipe the dairy mustache with his sleeve, I handed him a napkin. "Mommy can be bribed with kisses."

"Oh, you." I ruffled his hair. "Now you're giving away all of my secrets."

"Nuh uh, I didn't say you liked your feet rubbed."

"I'm up for kisses," Beau volunteered. Mesmerized, I watched his tongue slide out to catch a drop of syrup on his lower lip.

"I'm up for kisses, too." I wanted to crawl under the table at having verbalized my thoughts, but Beau acted as if I never said anything. The only indication he heard me was the twitch of a smile that threatened to end his attempt at indifference.

"Kiss…kiss…kiss," Tommy chanted until a shadow loomed over the table.

"Did you say you wanted another kiss?" Greg Anderson stood next to me with a to-go container in his hand. He seemed to absorb the little family scene going on at our table. "Cheating on me already?" His usual playfulness was there. His voice was like a poodle skirt—cute, and sweet, and all swishy.

"Come on over here, Greg." Beau slid across the booth bench and patted the seat next to him. Shocking all of us, he pulled Greg's head toward him and gave him a big smooch on the cheek. Tommy giggled while Greg turned the color of crimson icing.

His fingers touched his cheek as if he was relishing the moment. I'd seen that look all day yesterday when the girls flirted with Beau and happened to trace their fingers over his shoulder. I imagined there were a lot of unwashed hands in Bell Mountain.

"What was that for?"

"I thought I was going to have to kick your butt for kissing my girl, now I won't."

"Oh, my God," Greg squealed. "What did I miss? Are you back together?" He let out a happy sigh. "My work is done."

While Beau confirmed with a nod, I shook my head no.

Greg watched us both. He nodded, then shook his head, then nodded, then shrugged. "What is it, yes or no?"

In unison, Beau and I shouted out the answer. I, of course, said no, but Beau declared a solid yes, and that's what Greg went with. Was there some kind of bro-code that demanded men stick together—safer in a pack and all that? In that moment, I considered Greg a traitor. He was no longer one of the girls. He had crossed over to the dark side.

"Turncoat," I sneered.

"All in the name of love, sweetheart. Gotta go, the boss is a real stickler for breaks." He picked up his container and smiled all the way to the door.

"Ready, champ?" Beau tossed several twenties on the table. I started to argue, but he gave me a look that could stop a truck. If Beau Tinsel wanted to toss his money around, who was I to stop him?

CHAPTER TEN

BEAU

Who knew that hanging lights could be so much fun? We had always hired someone to take care of ours, but working with Tommy was pure bliss. After he showed us the wish ornaments, he insisted on changing all the bulbs so they weren't in random order. He said that a pattern of red, green, and gold would make him happy, and I was all about making Tommy happy.

Once the strands were draped across the roof, we called for Mandy and made her close her eyes. Tommy mimicked a drum roll while I plugged in the end of the strand. I swear I saw the lights in the neighborhood flicker from the power draw of the old bulbs, but they paled in comparison to what shined forth from Tommy's expression.

Mandy jumped up and down and pulled me to her side. She tiptoed up and kissed me on the cheek. "Thank you."

Excited to be close to her, I held my tongue, hoping

my silence would allow the moment to last. When she stepped away, my heart sank. "He says these are his first outside Christmas lights."

"It's true. We live in a small apartment in the city. What about you? Do you put lights up every year?"

"I never get around to it. Usually, I'm on the road."

Tommy tugged at Beau's hand. "Thanks, Beau, for being my friend."

I bent down and picked him up. Seeing him so excited made my heart twist. This was what perfection looked like, and I'd tossed it away out of a sense of obligation to do right. I had to get Mandy to trust me, to trust that I could be a good man for her, a good man for Tommy. I couldn't bear being away from her, from them. There had been too much distance already—ten years and thousands of miles.

Tears ran down her cheek. Were they happy or sad? I couldn't tell. She swiped at them.

"You okay?"

"There's something in my eye, can you take Tommy in?"

I thumbed the tears from her cheeks. "I've got him. I've got you too if you'd let me." Oh, how I wished she'd let me, but I already made too many decisions that hadn't been good for either of us. Taking me back had to be her choice. I'd tease—I'd poke—I'd prod, but I wouldn't force anything on her again.

She leaned into my touch. "I wish I could." She kissed my palm and ran to the door. When Tommy and I entered the house, she was already upstairs, and I could hear the soft muffles of her cry.

"Hey, buddy, your mom is tired. How about you and I go across the street to get my guitar. I'll give you your first lesson." Tommy didn't need much coaxing. He was back in his coat and hat and standing at the door in minutes.

Normally, I would have marched him across the street without thinking, but I was trying to be more aware of my actions with regard to Mandy and her wishes. She asked me to take Tommy in, but that didn't mean I had the right to abscond with him.

"Will I be able to play something after my first lesson?" Tommy pulled on his gloves, getting two fingers stuck in one finger space.

"Let's make that our goal." I tugged his glove off and put it back on, making sure only one finger took up residence for each space. "Stay here for a second, okay? I want to ask your mom if it's okay for me to take you to my house."

"She'll say yes. She trusts you."

If only that were true. "I'm working on her trust, Tommy, so I think it's best if I ask. You can come with me or you can wait right here."

He leaned against the door and slid to the ground. "I'll wait," he said before he plopped his head on his knees. Oh, to be a child again. Waiting was the worst thing in the world. I remember ordering my first guitar and sitting by the door for a week hoping it would show up. To a kid, five minutes was a lifetime.

"I'll hurry."

I dashed up the stairs and tapped on the second door to my right. When there wasn't an answer, I knocked a bit louder. "Mandy?" I turned the knob and stepped into her room. My girl was curled on her side under the pink canopy. She looked like a big kid in that bed.

It didn't seem so long ago that I'd crawled up the tree outside her window and snuck inside. It wasn't that I had to sneak in; Annie was always very open-minded about our relationship. I snuck in because it seemed more romantic. One of my best-selling singles was called "Through Your Window," and chronicled a boy's love for a girl. I began to sing the lyrics, "I'd fall any day for you. Any way for you. You are the window to my soul."

"What time is it?" She shot up to a sitting position. "I'm so sorry."

"Shhh, you've only been asleep for a couple minutes." I sat on the mattress next to her and stroked the strands of hair that had fallen in her face. "I just wanted to ask if I could take Tommy across the street for a guitar lesson?"

She flopped down on the mattress, her hair fanned across the pillow. She looked so damn sexy. "Were you just singing?"

"Yep, I wrote, 'Through Your Window' about us. In fact, all of the songs I've ever written are about you or us. You have always been my muse, Mandy." This would have been the perfect time to lean in and kiss her, but I didn't. Instead, I pulled the bedspread over her body and tucked it under her chin. "You rest while Tommy and I hang out."

"You don't have to babysit." She tried to push up,

91

but I laid my hand on her shoulder and pressed her back to the mattress.

"I want to hang out with him. It's not like he's a bother, and he wants to play guitar. I couldn't ask for a better afternoon. Let me do this," I pleaded.

What little fight she had left inside of her disappeared. Her tense muscles relaxed into the bed. She looked exhausted, and why wouldn't she be. She was dealing with a time change, the stress with me, a small boy who I'm sure could wear out the Energizer Bunny, and the Sweet Shop. It was a lot to take in.

"Make sure he behaves. Don't spoil him. No sweets." She reached out and pulled my hand to her lips. "I've always loved that song, by the way."

"I've always loved you." It took everything in me to get up and leave, but there was a six-year-old waiting downstairs, and I was sure his patience was wearing thin.

CHAPTER ELEVEN

MANDY

How was I supposed to process his statement? *"I've always loved you?"* Well, he sure had a fine way of showing it. Years of nothing, not even a call, and now he's back, and he tells me he loves me. Heat rushed to my face, but it wasn't from anger. It was from desire. The way he looked at me. The way he sang that song— a song I'd played every day for years. His smell. His gentle touch. Those damn blue eyes. Beau Tinsel was killing me cell by cell, starting in my heart.

I searched beneath my mattress until I came up with the binder I'd spent months compiling. Every article or picture I could find was cut and pasted into a scrapbook of sorts. I'd kissed his pictures and ex'ed out the faces of anyone near. It didn't matter if it was a waiter, a waitress, or a hot blonde model. My eyes only had room for him.

As I flipped the pages, I revisited every victory and every defeat from the day he left to the day he called and said he wasn't coming home. I'd written his words on the last page between the two halves of my favorite picture of us. My fingers traced the words that sliced straight through my heart.

I know I promised to come back for you, but I can't right now. Things are complicated. Nothing is like I thought it would be. I want it to be more. I don't want you in this life. Those were his words but did I listen to the message?

What I heard was, *I'm not coming back. I'm having too much fun being single. I want more of this, and you would only ruin things for me. I don't want you to be in my life.*

With love, I ran my fingers over the words. Years of maturity had changed their meaning. Clarity was an amazing thing. *I know I promised to come back for you, but I can't right now,* translated into, *I love you too much to allow you to follow me. Things are complicated. Nothing is like I thought it would be,* was actually, *I'm not sure if I'm making the right decision, but I have to think of you first. I want it to be more, I don't want you in this life* could only mean, *chase your dreams, I want more for you.*

With a groan, I flopped back onto my bed. God, I was an idiot. All these years, I'd avoided home and him because he talked in lyrical truths. I wanted to choke him and kiss him at the same time. Maybe I'd choke him first and then kiss him, or maybe I'd just kiss him.

I jumped from my bed and looked at myself in the mirror. *Oh, God, look at me.* There would be no kisses until I straightened my shit out. I'd been living in a Chef's coat and jeans for years. My hair had a permanent band mark from the ponytail I always wore. *Shit, shit, shit.*

With few options, I rummaged through my closet, and in the back corner, I found the perfect outfit to let

Beau Tinsel know I still cared. After I showered, I unearthed the blow dryer that was purchased my freshman year of high school. I said a silent prayer the minute I plugged it in, that the house wouldn't erupt into flames.

Naked in front of the mirror, I analyzed my body while I styled my hair. My breasts were heavy, my hips were wide, and my stomach bore the scars of mother-hood. Beau had left a taut teenager with perky tits and a flat stomach. Could he want me in my lesser state, or more accurately, my *more* state? *Oh hell, did it matter?* All that mattered was for us to bury the past. I didn't have any wild dreams of becoming Mrs. Tinsel, but I did want to be his friend. I wanted him to like me again, really like me.

After I applied the mascara I rarely wore, I smiled at the girl who had been hidden for so long. It had been a while since I'd seen her staring back at me from the mirror. She'd disappeared in a relentless work schedule, thousands of diaper changes, and sleepless nights. But today, my eyes were bright and happy-looking. Beau used to tell me my eyes were flawless emeralds. We used to joke about how our babies would look with one sapphire blue eye from him, and one emerald eye from me. In the end, we decided our children would be born with topaz-colored eyes because ruby eyes and multiple-colored eyes would be too freaky. That was before we really considered DNA and dominant genes.

Dressed in what used to be Beau's football jersey, I took one last look in the mirror. The white numbers were like hands squeezing my breasts. Number ten had been my lucky number for years. The irony of the number didn't escape me either.

Mom and Sarah were entering the front door as I trotted down the stairs. Both of them took in my outfit, my make-up, and my demeanor. It was obvious they were pleased by their grins.

"Wow, you look great," said Sarah. "So…things are going well with Beau?" I could feel her hope, it danced in the air like electricity.

"We don't hate each other anymore." I tugged at the jersey, feeling naked under the scrutiny. Was it too much to be wearing his number again?

Speak of the devil himself. Beau and Tommy burst through the door. In Beau's hand was his old guitar— covered with stickers of all kinds. I'd put half of them on myself. My favorite was the "girls rule" sticker. I'd scribbled out "girls" and written in "Mandy." It was still there, taking up prime real estate.

The Grandmas directed Tommy into the kitchen. When they said they were going to teach him how to make spaghetti, he said, "I charge five dollars for my cooking services."

"Tommy," I warned in my don't-be-a-brat voice.

"Okay, half-price for you both." I kneeled down and gave him a kiss. It didn't matter how long he was gone, be it five minutes or five hours, I always missed him.

"Go help your grandmothers." I looked up at Beau when I included his mother in the mix. He was right; it didn't take DNA to make a family. With a gentle swat to his bottom, I sent Tommy on his way.

Beau looked at his jersey and smiled. I'd worn it with

pride for every game of every season. "You still look as good as ever, Mandy." When his tongue slid out to wet his lips, my knees grew weak.

"I am extremely limited on stuff to wear." I played it off like I hadn't done laundry in weeks, which wasn't far from the truth, but those piles were still in the corner of my apartment. When mom had called, I'd packed what was clean and we ran out the door.

"And I thought you were sending a message."

"Maybe I am." *Yes, I still had it.* That flirty girl was fighting her way back out.

"I always loved you in my jersey, but I loved you out of it more." He stalked toward me, step by slow step until I was forced to look up to him.

I grabbed hold of the banister for balance. My knees shook under my faded blue jeans. I may be able to flirt a bit, but I was way out of my element here. Beau had been with probably hundreds of women, I'd been with one man since he'd left. This wasn't high school, and Beau was in a totally different league.

"I can't do this." I whipped around to head up the stairs, but he stopped me. He pulled me close, burying his nose in that sensitive place on my shoulder. He didn't kiss me, he just held me for a long minute.

"Don't go." His breath whispered against my neck, making the hairs on my arms tingle and stand. "Let's talk about what you think you can't do." He sat on the first step and tugged me down beside him. His fingers skimmed the sleeve of the jersey.

With a huff of frustration, I spilled out my first concern. "I feel inadequate. I'm not rail thin, I'm not model beautiful." It was out. I'd never considered my looks before. It had always been Beau and me, so jealousy never bled from me like it did each time I saw him with another beauty.

He pulled his guitar from where he'd leaned it on the wall minutes before and began to strum a few chords of his hit single, "You Never Forget Your First."

"You were my first everything, Mandy. I wrote that song for you. I've written every song for you. Do you know what the second verse is?"

I nodded and sang the words. "Beginning, middle and end, you are the one I'll always love. You're my forever love." I'll be damned if I wasn't going to have to listen to every one of his songs again with fresh ears.

"That's right. Who do you think is my forever love?"

I scrunched my nose and groaned. "Piper Williams?" She was another model who had decorated his arm several times.

"Come here, you." He leaned his guitar against the wall and pulled my head into his chest where he proceeded to knuckle my hair. "Let me tell you about Piper Williams. Her name is Elle Waterhouse, and she's my agent's niece. She needed more exposure, so I accompanied her to a few fashion shows. Most boring time of my life."

"Did you kiss her?"

"No, she's like eighteen. Give me some credit, Mandy. She's a baby."

"She's legal, which is more than I can say for half the groupies. Look what happened to you at the Sweet Shop. You're a teenager's dream."

"You know why? It's because I sing about teenage love. The kind of love that when it goes wrong wrings out your heart. I sing about us."

"Every song is about us?"

"Yes, name a song and I'll tell you the history."

I sat back so I could see his eyes. Everything was always in his eyes. Right now, they were filled with optimism and longing. "Reckless." I crossed my hands over my chest and waited.

He tossed his head and gave me a that's-easy look. "Do you know the verse that begins with, *So wrong for the right reasons*? Right after I heard you were pregnant, I reevaluated my decisions. My heart had been in the right place, but I'd been so wrong, and I'd lost you. I'd been reckless."

"I was pregnant, not married."

"Mandy, you were always the marrying kind. I couldn't imagine you with a child and not a husband. You wanted the house, the picket fence, and the two-point-five kids. I got a wallop the other night from my mom when I brought up the subject of you being married. I was filling in the blanks with my own story, not the real story."

"It would seem we both have been doing a lot of assuming."

I went over the lyrics to "Sideline Girl" in my head. "Oh, my God, 'Sideline Girl' was about football, not a girl on the side."

"No, it was about you in the stands wearing my number." He sang the first line of the chorus, "*she's a ten in every way*, And you are. You were then, but now…"

I held my breath waiting for his report card. What was his grading system like these days? "I'm what?" I wanted to blurt out, *a high five on a scale of ten*? But I no longer wanted to make assumptions.

"You're an eleven and when you beg me to kiss you, you'll be a twelve." He rolled forward and stood up. "Should we go save Tommy from the Grandmas?"

I wanted to pull him back down and kiss him, but I wasn't ready to beg—yet. I was still processing everything he said. So, he'd always loved me; I'd always loved him. That hadn't changed, but so many other things had.

CHAPTER TWELVE

BEAU

"He's a natural," my voice boomed with pride. "He can already play G, C, and D, which means he can just about play any song unless they're angsty and require a maudlin minor chord." I passed the bowl of meatballs to Tommy who was sporting his own pride by way of a wide smile.

"We wrote a song together." A piece of spaghetti hung from his chin until I plucked it away.

"You little stinker, that was supposed to be a surprise."

His bright smile fell to a frown. "Oh no, I forgot."

Every eye looked to me to see how I would handle this situation. Hell, it didn't take Einstein to know that Tommy felt bad, and I didn't want that at all. Tommy was a little boy, and little boys needed to feel good. It was part of confidence building.

"It's all right, champ. Some surprises are so exciting they bubble out before we can pull the words back. Tell them about your song." I gave him a pat on the back for encouragement.

He bounced in his seat. "It's called 'Peppermint Kisses' and it's about a boy and a girl having a fight over which is better."

Mandy laughed. "Peppermint of course."

"No, Mommy, that's not how the song goes. It says they're better together."

I dared to look up at Mandy. Her emerald greens danced with warmth I hadn't seen in a long time.

Annie cleared her throat, which ended our private moment. "I have to drive to Denver the day after tomorrow. The orthopedic doctor called and wants to discuss my MRI. Oh, and Alliance called and said your car is ready. It was a loose battery cable. No charge."

"Wow, I would have sworn it was the starter by the clunking sound. Do you need a ride to Denver?" I offered.

"Oh, goodness no, your mom and I are going to go together. We thought we'd take Tommy with us so we can do some last minute Christmas shopping."

"I have five dollars to buy presents." Tommy whipped the wrinkled bill from the front pocket of his jeans and waved it around. "Is it enough to buy Mommy a diamond?"

"Mommy never asked for a diamond. She doesn't need one," Mandy said.

"Grandma's song says diamonds are a girl's best friend." He swirled spaghetti on his fork and continued. "Mommy doesn't have any friends. I want her to have a best friend."

"Mom, must you play all those old songs for him? Before you know it, he'll be wanting Santa baby to hurry down my chimney tonight." Mandy closed her eyes and rubbed above the bridge of her nose while we all cracked up. She tapped the table to quiet the raucous. "Tommy, look at me. Things can't be friends. You can appreciate and desire things, but they can never take the place of a friend." She looked around the table; her eyes stopped at me. "Good friends are with you for life."

"Okay," he said with a pout to his voice. "But you'd like a diamond if I bought you one, right?"

"Yes, Tommy, I like diamonds, but you'll need more than five dollars to buy a diamond. Why don't you make me something instead?"

He slumped back in his chair and crossed his arms in a mood. "I should have charged the Grandmas to cook."

"Tell you what, buddy, you and I will figure something out for your mom, okay?"

The Grandmas' heads bounced as they looked between Mandy, Tommy, and me.

"Oh no, you don't," Mandy scowled at me. "He has to earn his money just like everyone else."

"He tried, but you wouldn't let him charge the grannies." She knew I had a point because her head fell forward in defeat.

"Tommy, Grandma Sarah and I will pay you five dollars to help us clean up the mess." Annie looked at my mom and nodded toward the kitchen. "Let them straighten out their *family* matters alone."

Tommy cleared off his classic car placemat and

skipped into the kitchen behind our meddlesome mothers.

"You better watch out or those two will have us married and living next door." She cupped her hand to her mouth like she was trying to spoon back the words.

"There are worse fates than marrying me, Mandy."

"Really?" she teased, "tell me one."

"You could marry old Tom from the drugstore?" By the horror on her face, I hit my mark.

"Eww, how could you even say that? Yuck. He used to leer at me when I bought condoms. I went on the pill because of him."

"I thought you went on the pill because of me."

"You know what I mean." She leaned in and whispered, "the man eye-sexed me each time I went in there." She squirmed in her seat like she had ants in her pants.

"The term is," I glanced around to make sure Tommy wasn't in hearing distance, "eye-fucked and just about everyone did that to you in high school. How do you think I got all those bloody knuckles and so many guys had black eyes?"

Recognition dawned on her face. "I thought it was from football practice."

"You don't understand the allure of your beauty. It's inside and out, Mandy. I loved the way you looked, but I loved the sweetness and innocence that was your soul."

"And now?" She drew her thumb to her mouth and bit at her fingernail.

"I'm going to love you all over again if you'd just give me a chance."

"But I'm jaded and frayed around the edges."

I wanted to rush to her side and pull her into my arms. "You're like an apple in its prime. You've matured and ripened, not rotted. You're still sweet but just a little bruised." I could see the doubt on her face, and I knew that I could kiss it away, but I promised myself the next time I tasted her lips would be on her terms.

"I've been called a lot of things, but never an apple." She pushed away from the table and turned to walk toward the living room. My name was emblazoned on her back. By Christmas, it would be embedded in her heart. That was the promise I made to myself.

Seconds later, three troublemakers walked out of the kitchen. The plate of cookies and the tray of hot cocoa my mom held gave me an idea.

"Tommy, I know of a perfect way you can earn money." Every eye snapped in my direction. Annie and my mom took the single seats, forcing Mandy, Tommy, and I to share the couch.

"How much do you think I can earn?" He sat up straight. "Enough to buy a diamond?"

Mandy let out an exasperated groan. "Enough about the diamond."

"This will take the help of everyone, so here's my thought. Can Tommy and I have the corner table of the Sweet Shop tomorrow from three to five?"

All three women passed looks of puzzlement between them, but it was Mandy who answered. "Sure, what do you need it for?"

Mimicking Tommy's stature, I sat tall and presented my business plan. "BT's...Beau and Tommy's hot cocoa stand. I figured if Mom made the cocoa, and Tommy and I sold it in the corner, all you would need to do is make more cookies because you can't buy hot chocolate and not match it up with a cookie. Now, it may cut into your cocoa sales, but it's for a good cause, and half of what Tommy takes in will be donated to a charity of his choice."

"Half?" Tommy looked appalled. He already had a head for business. Half was ridiculous, but I'd always made it a point to give half of everything I earned to charity. You could only use so much money, but gratitude was something worth more than the dollars that would collect in my bank account.

"Yes, half is a lot, but think about all the people you could help with your donation. What do you *really* like, Tommy?"

He sat in contemplation for under a minute. "I like music."

"Okay, so you can donate half to the music program at the high school, and I'll match whatever you donate. Those programs struggle to survive, especially in small towns. You can make a difference."

His grin grew from a crack to a crater. He tossed out his hand to shake. "Deal."

"Not so fast, buddy, we need help from these fine women. Grandma Sarah needs to make her special hot cocoa, and Grandma Annie needs to give her okay since the shop belongs to her. Then, you need the most important yes to come from your mother." Tommy and I put our puppy dog expressions on and waited.

"I'll be happy to make the cocoa and donate the

ingredients." I hadn't seen my mom so happy in years. Sure, she was always overjoyed to see me when she visited, but this was different. This felt like family, which was something none of us had really embraced for years. I'd wasted so much time.

Annie donated the cups and gave us her full support. Mandy, on the other hand, looked at us in the same way a librarian did when you made noise. She pursed her lips and narrowed her eyes.

Tommy began to tap his foot in impatience, but he never said a word.

"I have a few conditions before I give my approval."

I leaned toward Tommy, "This is called a negotiation, buddy. Your mom will ask for concessions and then we'll counter with our demands. This goes back and forth until someone comes out the victor." The poor kid looked at me like he'd lost me at the word "your." "Can I negotiate on your behalf?"

Tommy gave an enthusiastic nod.

"Name your demands, Ms. Sawyer."

She adjusted herself so she was facing us directly.

"Number one, Tommy has to do the work. Number two, he has to help with the cleanup. Number three, at five o'clock, we close up shop and go out to Big Jim's for barbecue. My treat."

"Yes. Yes. Yes," Tommy repeated.

"Tommy, you can't give in on the first round. We had an opportunity to negotiate."

Tommy sat his hand on my knee. "We got everything we wanted and dinner out."

I shook my head at the precocious young man next to me. "I have one demand. I pay."

"Deal," Tommy shouted.

"Now you're negotiating for me?" Mandy shook her head. "Go get that guitar, young man. I want to hear about those peppermint kisses."

CHAPTER THIRTEEN

MANDY

Corralling an excited six-year-old was like trying to catch a slippery fish. The hot cocoa brigade arrived just before three with Tommy about to jump out of his skin. The only good thing about his excess energy was that he'd sleep well tonight.

Misty and I had set up the corner with cups and a cash box. We had prepared the boys for success. A huge silver coffee urn filled with warm cocoa sat in the corner waiting for Tommy to serve. All that was missing were his customers. I hoped this wouldn't be a big disappointment for my son, but if it were, it would be a learning opportunity.

"Let's take our picture, and let people know we're here." Beau raised his phone and shot a picture of Tommy and him scrunched together in the corner. Then, he posted it on every social media site known to man. "See here, Tommy," he held up the selfie. "It says, Help Tommy's stocking fund, come for the cocoa, and stay for the music. Half of the donations will be donated to the Bell Mountain High School music department." He pulled his guitar from the corner and began to strum some Christmas tunes starting with "Peppermint Kisses." I leaned on the counter and stared at him like a star-struck fan. *Sweet as candy but not as sweet as Mandy*, his silly lyrics made me smile. I'd missed his music. I'd missed his company. I'd just plain missed him.

By three-thirty, the shop was swarming with screaming girls and a few boys, too. Tommy poured cocoa while Beau smiled and played for his adoring fans. Sarah was in the back making her second batch of hot chocolate, while Mom tried to snap pictures one-handed. Her poor wrist was in worse shape than I thought. She'd become quite an accomplished left-hander since her accident. Mom was a survivor.

After Misty and I had been relieved of duty by the two teens pulling the closing shift, we stood against the wall and watched the chaos unfold. Each time an overzealous fan got too friendly, I tensed, and if Theresa Platt didn't stop bending over Beau to push her boobs into his face, she'd have a black eye, and I'd have the bruised and bloody knuckles. I saw the way she was looking at him, and that couldn't be construed as anything but eye-fucking.

Five o'clock took forever to get here, but when it did, I slammed the front doors shut and locked the fans outside. Still, their noses pressed to the windows to get a last glimpse at my boys.

Tommy made six hundred and forty-three dollars in

donations, half of which would go to the school, and the remaining half would be split between opening a savings account for him and his Christmas shopping fund. It was so cute that he wanted to give me a diamond, but in all honesty, I wasn't the kind of girl who needed jewels to feel rich. I'd found immense wealth in the love and affection of a six-year-old boy.

Tommy and Beau cleaned up their corner. They both looked exhausted. Tommy was worn threadbare by the experience, whereas the crowds seemed to suck the energy right out of Beau. I'd never considered his job to be taxing, he was always doing what he loved, but there was so much more than playing a guitar and singing pretty words to be a superstar. Everyone wanted a piece of him, including me.

We evaded the lurking fans and snuck through the back door to slip into Big Jim's Barbecue across the street. Once inside, I insisted we sit in the dark corner so no one would notice Beau and interrupt our dinner. Our chatty mothers weren't paying any attention to us. They were planning their trip to Denver tomorrow. They were Thelma and Louise without the cliff.

"How do you do it?" I lifted my hand to his face and rubbed at the dark circles under his eyes. He leaned into my palm. The heat between us rushed through my body.

Tommy had squeezed in the center, creating an unwelcome but lovable barrier. His head leaned into Beau as his little eyes bobbed up and down until they gave up and closed.

"It's part of the gig. I don't love the crowds, but without the fans, I have no one to play for." Beau cradled Tommy's head into his chest as if it were the most natural action to take. Each time I saw them together, my heart softened and took in the love around me. I feared by the end of the week, it might burst having grown too big for my chest cavity.

"You can play for me." I thought of all the private concerts Beau had given me. Most nights, he had climbed the tree outside my room and slid into my unlocked window. I always knew when he was coming because he'd leave that old stickered guitar in my room. It was a giddy feeling, knowing he was on his way, but never knowing when he'd show.

"I will play for you." He looked at me with heat in his eyes—the kind of heat that boiled from my heart to my pink parts.

"Can I get you something to drink?" A look of recognition crossed our waitress' face when she looked at Beau.

I waved her in close. "Can you not tell anyone he's here? I promise you a big tip, and I'm pretty sure he'll autograph anything you want."

Her brows lifted to her blunt cut bangs. "Anything?" I nodded and shooed her away.

Beau covered Tommy's exposed ear with his palm. "You realize I'm going to be signing her ass or her boobs, right?"

I sucked in the air around me. "No way. Who does that?" We both turned to look at the waitress who, at that moment, was adjusting her cleavage. In unison, we said, "her."

"How many people ask you to sign their boobs?" At the word "boobs," both of our moms stopped talking and stared.

"Yes, Beau," Sarah said. "How many do you sign?"

"I'm not talking about this here." All three of us drilled him with questioning gazes. The poor man was stuck in the corner and pinned by our eyes. "All right, lots, but I don't enjoy it." That little twitch to his lip gave him away.

"Right, it's like a candy store at every concert, and you don't enjoy the sweets?" I rolled my eyes at him and hid my jealousy behind the menu.

"At first, it was mind-blowing, but then, not so much."

"Hmm, I bet more than your mind got blown," I mumbled, hoping our mothers didn't hear me.

He pulled the menu down to look at me. Our mothers looked on like smiling loons.

"Jealous?" I watched his mouth form the word, and when he got to the "L" and his tongue nestled between his teeth, I was captivated by how wet, and red, and suckaliscious it was. He leaned in and pulled the menu up to shelter us. "Mandy, your lips are the only ones that can blow me…away."

A whisper of air flushed over my skin, causing goosebumps to rise on my flesh. Everything in my body screamed yes, from the heat between my legs to my painfully-pebbled nipples, but I said no. "No, not here."

"When...where?" Desperation rasped his voice.

Just to get him off my back, or at least, that's what I told myself, I pecked him on the lips real quick. A tremor rushed through me. It felt like a tiny little orgasm, gone too quickly and not enough to satisfy my craving for this man.

"Is that all I get?"

"Yes." We were still behind the menu, but I could feel our mothers' eyes on us. I never inherited the x-ray vision that most mothers seemed to possess, but I knew both of our mothers had it. They always knew what we were up to. I widened my eyes and tossed my head in their direction as if to say, "They're staring at us."

He leaned in closer, his whiskers rubbed against my neck, "I don't care. What you gave me was like a single sprinkle when I'm craving the whole decorated cookie."

"Overindulging is not good for anyone," I tossed back.

"Neither is starving for ten years."

"You're crushing me," Tommy whined. "I'm hungry." He wormed his way into a sitting position and pulled the menu down, which confirmed my suspicions. The moms were all ears and grins.

"Hey champ, your mom and me were just deciding what we wanted for dessert." Beau gave me that I-want-you look he had perfected long ago. "Sometimes, it's better to choose your dessert first, that way, you can make smart choices beforehand. Why would you eat big if what you really want is the cookie?"

"With sprinkles," my mother shouted while Sarah

laughed. "Kids...they think they invented menus for privacy. These two have a lot to learn."

I wanted to kick them under the table, but in all honesty, it felt like old times when Beau and I would sneak kisses and share words of affection. Our mothers knew and supported our relationship. It broke their hearts, the way things had gone, but here we were, back at the beginning—again. No, I corrected my thoughts. This wasn't the beginning, but maybe a new chapter of a follow-on book.

"I want a hot dog and a hot fudge sundae." Tommy snuggled against my arm, and I embraced him.

"Let's order, then." Glad to change the subject from sexual innuendo to food, I raised my hand to get the attention of our waitress. She bounced over to our table and took our order.

"I got my pen ready." She looked over the group then zeroed in on Beau. "Is this your sister?"

"No, sweetheart," he leaned toward her, grabbed the pen from her hand, and scribbled his name across her palm, "this woman's my everything." He held up his near-empty glass of water. "I'd love a refill, please." His eyes turned toward me, and I knew tonight, he'd get whatever he wanted. I'd never been claimed like that before in my life. If our moms weren't here and Tommy wasn't sitting between us, I would have pulled him from the booth and dragged him home. Hunger be damned.

After racks of ribs, brisket, and barbecued chicken, we were fat and almost happy. Tommy was scraping the bottom of his sundae while Beau pulled two hundreds from his wallet.

"That's a big tip."

"It's her consolation."

"What, for not getting her you-know-what signed?"

"No, for realizing she never had a chance." Beau tapped Tommy to get him moving. "Let's go. I think there's a cookie in my future."

CHAPTER FOURTEEN

BEAU

Mandy sat in the passenger seat, twisting her fingers in her lap. I don't ever remember her being so nervous. "You okay?"

"Yeah…sure." She stopped pretzeling her fingers and fumbled with the radio buttons until she found a song she recognized. "I'm nervous."

I pulled the car over. Tommy had gone home with the Grandmas to get a bath and a story before bedtime so no one was counting on us for anything. When I cut the engine, I turned toward her. "You don't have to be nervous. I want a lot of things from you, but I'd never demand anything."

"It's not you, it's me. I'm not the same girl. I told you, everything has changed." She cupped her beautiful breasts. "Even these wouldn't get a passing grade on your old scale."

God, I wanted to cup her breasts and tell her how perfect they were. "Can I?" I reached toward her hands.

She chewed the inside of her cheek and nodded. I

was back to being sixteen and sitting on her bed when I first felt her up. We were a tangle of limbs and lips, and I'd never been so happy.

With caution, I cupped her hands in mine and felt the weight of her breasts. She dropped her palms, leaving the entire experience in my hands completely. Through her bra, I could feel the strain of her nipples as I brushed my thumbs across the thin cotton of her shirt. She hissed when I circled the hard nubs. "They're perfect, Mandy. I wouldn't care if you had nipples on a board, or your tits sagged to your knees. I'm drawn to you. I want you, and only you."

"Kiss me, Beau, and make me believe you."

I hated the big console between us. There was no finessing this kiss, it was offered and would be taken. There were ten years of unfulfilled passion to satisfy. That was a huge expectation for one kiss. With one hand on her right breast and one weaved through the strands of her hair, I gripped the nape of her neck and pulled her to me. This kiss meant more because she'd asked for it.

Hot, greedy lips reached for mine. I suckled and nipped and caressed her mouth. With a gentle pull, I coaxed her quivering lower lip between mine and ran my tongue over the plump length. She shuddered, so I gripped her tight, trying to silently communicate to her that I had her and that I'd take care of her.

Little gasps and moans slipped between us. I was halfway over the center console before I noticed the flashing lights behind us.

Thump.

Thump.

Thump.

"Shit," Mandy yelled as she struggled to pull herself together. Her hair was in disarray, her lips were kiss-swollen, and her T-shirt had been pulled up. The cup of her bra was pushed to the side and her rose-colored nipple exposed.

"It's okay." I adjusted her clothing first before I made any attempts to hide my straining erection. Not even the tails of my shirt could camouflage the solid rod between my legs.

Thump.

Thump.

Thump.

I rolled down the fogged window to find Sheriff Lerner leaning in with his hand on his holster.

"Well, look who's here," he said with a cowboy twang. "I heard you were back in town." He looked past me to Mandy. "Mandy, good to see you. Misty says you're back at the shop?"

She cleared her throat and ran her fingers through her hair. "Yes, sir. I'm helping out my mom." She sat straight as a ruler, facing forward.

"You got car problems?" The Sheriff was no dummy. His shit-eating grin was all too familiar. We'd been in this situation about twelve years ago. I'd pulled into the lookout and lost track of everything around us until he came knocking, just like tonight. It's a wonder any kid got past second base in this town. Sheriff Lerner was everywhere.

"No…no car problems."

"So, what are you two doing parked in the dark on the side of the road with your windows fogged?"

"Talking, Sheriff," Mandy fidgeted a bit more, "we have a lot of catching up to do. We were just talking."

"Is that what you're calling it these days?"

"We'll be going now, Sheriff. Thanks for stopping by to say hello." I pressed the ignition button and the SUV purred to life.

"There are better places to 'talk' you two. I hear Whitley's has a few vacancies." His chest bounced with hearty laughter. "Stay inside and stay warm, it's supposed to snow tomorrow."

"Thanks, Sheriff." I rolled up the window, turned up the defroster, and waited for the windows to clear.

"That was embarrassing. You'd think we were still teens with the way we were behaving. I have a six-year-old for goodness sake."

"It was fun, though. I felt like a teenager again. The kiss was amazing." She rocked her head back and forth. "Don't tell me you didn't think that was amazing?" I pinched her chin between my thumb and finger and pulled her to the center. "Tell me you didn't think that was the most amazing kiss ever?"

"It was good, but I'm counting on better. Now, take me home, Beau. I don't want the Sheriff to catch us again and call my mother." Lord, what would her mother have said to that? Somehow, she would have turned it into her victory. After the death of Mandy's dad, Annie had controlled everything she could. Who could blame her when all of our lives had spiraled so far out of control that day?

Our fingers intertwined the whole way home. Life was getting better every second. The biggest hurdle was getting Mandy to leave everything and come to California with me.

When we walked into the house, Tommy was sitting in his Spiderman pajamas with my guitar in his lap, practicing his chords.

"What took you so long?" He ran to us both and curled one arm around each of our legs.

"Yes, what took you so long?" Annie emerged from the kitchen with a cup of something in her hand. "Tommy was waiting."

I gave Mandy a knowing look. "We ran into Sheriff Lerner on the way." I played it off like it was a normal occurrence.

"He was just hanging out on the road home? That's odd."

"Mom, stop it." Mandy turned the color of a pomegranate. "We stopped and—"

"I know, and I'm glad you two are figuring it out."

Mandy mumbled something about x-ray vision and then smothered Tommy in kisses.

"Tommy wanted a goodnight song instead of a story, are you up for that, Beau?"

"It sounds like I'm up." I set the guitar aside and threw a giggling Tommy over my shoulder. "Where's my mom?"

Annie took her cup and sat in the chair next to the Christmas tree. Its branches sagged under the weight of the ornaments. "She went home to get ready for our trip."

"You know, Mom," Mandy started, "I can ask one of the teens to fill in tomorrow so I can go to your appointment."

"No, I want you at the shop. If that had been a viable option, I could have done that myself. They can sell, they can't bake."

I reached for my guitar while I balanced a wiggly boy over my shoulder. "I can fill in. I can't bake but I can try."

"Young man, with the crowds you bring, poor Misty would be withered by noon." I couldn't argue there. If a kid could make over six hundred dollars in donations, I couldn't imagine what would happen if I were behind the counter without Mandy for any length of time. "You're probably right."

Mandy kicked her feet up on the coffee table. "Sheriff Lerner says it's supposed to snow tomorrow. Do you think it's wise to drive down the pass?"

"You may be a mom, but you're not my mom." Annie sipped her tea. Her eyes crinkled with happiness as the warm liquid went down. Annie loved her tea. I remember her and Mandy's dad sitting in front of the bay window every night drinking tea and talking about their day. Like my parents, they had a good marriage. "We'll be fine, besides, it's too cold to snow. It's still subzero."

I left the two women to argue over the chance of snow and carried Tommy to his room. *Plop*, I dumped him onto the plaid comforter. He scurried under the covers and turned on his side.

"Do you love my mommy?"

How did I explain to a little boy that I'd been in love with his mother longer than he'd been alive?

"I've always loved your mom, but sometimes, we men aren't all that smart when it comes to girls." I snuggled the blanket under his chin.

"I don't like girls."

"You'll change your mind." I pulled the guitar across my lap. "What do you want to hear?"

"Peppermint Kisses."

I played our silly little song and changed the lyrics so Tommy was as sweet as candy. It didn't rhyme as well as Mandy, but he seemed to like it. When his eyes grew heavy, I leaned in to give him a kiss on the cheek. To my surprise, he wrapped his little arms around my neck and tugged me down.

"I love you, Beau."

A lump big enough to choke me formed in my throat. "I love you too, buddy." How could I not love him, he was everything I'd want in a son? I dimmed his light and shut his door.

Before I headed downstairs, I walked into Mandy's room and left my guitar in the corner.

CHAPTER FIFTEEN

MANDY

W hen Beau came downstairs, he looked pleased with himself.

"Is he down?"

"Yep, he was tired out from the day. He's very excited about tomorrow's shopping trip." Beau slid next to me on the couch and rested his hand on my knee. Heat surged through me.

"You youngsters have a good night," Mom rocked to her feet and kissed us both on the cheek before she walked down the hallway. "Lock up before you head to bed," she said before she took the turn into her main-level bedroom.

"Will do, Mrs. Sawyer." Beau leaned back against the cushions and pulled me into his lap. He was nibbling on my ear in no time. I could feel his hard length beneath me. I loved that I could still get him hard. Here he was, a big star who could choose any woman, and yet, I was the one he wanted, at least, for now. It was both exhilarating and terrifying. I could think of a thousand reasons why I was wrong for him, but when he kissed me, it felt so right.

Somehow, my breasts found their way back into his hands and my tongue into his mouth. We breathed each other in while we reacquainted ourselves. I straddled him and ground into his hardness. We rocked together in harmony. Out of breath, I leaned back to gulp in much needed oxygen. His blue eyes were sex heavy and half closed. His lips were a lollipop red that begged for licking and tasting. His palms gripped my ass and pulled me tight against his erection. Moans and groans slipped between us like a common language.

His hands pressed between my jeans and ass, grazing my skin with fingertips calloused from years of guitar playing. Rough skin and his soft touch were the perfect combination.

"Hold tight, baby." He slid his palms from my jeans and gripped my hips to stop their rotation. "I'm not making love to you on the couch with your mom down the hallway, and I refuse to come in my pants, which I'm close to doing."

"Come upstairs." My wispy breath filled the silence. I wanted him back in every way. I needed him like a fish needed water.

"Not right now, love. Let's make a special date when our mom's get back tomorrow night. We can stay at the cabin and make love in front of the fireplace like old times. I'm sure my mom, or your mom, will watch Tommy."

Like a deflated balloon, I sagged against his chest. I

was burning like an ember ready to ignite but was doused with water instead.

"I just got you back." Each word was delivered with a silent plea for him to change his mind. "I'm begging, Beau."

"You don't need to beg, baby. You just need to wait. Our first time back together needs to be better than your mom's couch with both of us looking over our shoulders for Tommy."

He was right. Our desire was fierce. Enough so that it had taken away my common sense. I didn't want Tommy walking in while I rode Beau, and I didn't want my mother to get an eyeful either. I preached patience to my son all the time, the least I could do was set an example, if only to myself.

"What now?" I rested my head on his broad chest. Beau had always been a big guy. Tall and muscular, he was every woman's dream and every man's nightmare. Ten years had passed, and yet, the muscles he had in high school were still there. I ran my fingertips over each ridge and ripple, reminding myself of the man I'd loved for so long.

"I'm going to give you one more panty-twisting kiss, and then, I'm leaving you." He cupped my face and in his eyes, I saw love—years of lost love now found.

"Do you have to leave?" Pathetic in my attempt to coax him to stay, I owed it to myself to capture every minute, even if we sat here on the couch and stared at the powder blue walls.

"I have to call my agent. He's working on something

that could be big. I was supposed to call him earlier, but my mouth was otherwise occupied."

His goodbye kiss was tender and sweet. Rather than ravish me with a bruising touch, he lingered and loved me. That kiss was more intimate than any lovemaking session I could remember. Ten years ago, we were clumsy teenagers doing what came naturally. These days, I had to imagine lovemaking would be done with more skill and finesse than we were capable of back then.

I watched him walk across the street, and even though I knew he couldn't see me in the darkened window, he had to have felt my eyes on him. When he reached his door, he turned and blew me a kiss that I felt in the deepest recesses of my heart.

When I turned around, Mom was standing there with unbridled joy written all over her face. "Things going well?"

I rushed to her and threw my arms around her. "I should throttle you for your interference, but all I can say is thank you. We have a long road ahead, but at least we are traveling it together. I don't know what will happen, Mom, but thanks for bringing Beau back into my life."

"I didn't fall to get you or Beau here, however, once I did, a lot of options opened up." Mom held me a moment longer than normal. She held me the way I held Tommy. This was the mom I'd longed for and in that moment, her arms seemed stronger than Superman, her compassion more than Mother Theresa, and her cunning could give the most talented con artist a run for his money.

"I love you, Mom. You know I'd do anything for you." I kissed her cheek and inhaled the scent of her Pond's face cream. For years, I'd been frustrated with my mom for living in the past, for never trying new things, for not moving forward after my father died, for controlling everything around her—including me.

Here I had been doing the same thing. Sure, I was living at its basic level, but I'd stopped loving because Beau Tinsel had stolen my heart, and had hidden it for a decade. Now, it was free, and that made me feel higher than the bottle of bubbly I'd drunk by myself last New Year's Eve.

We separated, with Mom going to bed, and me heading upstairs. I peeked in on Tommy. He was curled in a ball, his little lower lip puffed out with each breath. Not everything over the last ten years had been bad. I'd traveled across Europe, worked with the finest pastry chefs and chocolatiers in the world, and I'd had Tommy. Sitting on the edge of his bed, I rubbed his back and thanked the lucky stars Beau had let me go.

Trying to imagine my life without Tommy was impossible. He'd been my life for years. He brought laughter and joy to everything. He'd taught me about sacrifice, and the importance of serving others needs first. Parents are supposed to teach their children, but I wonder if it's not the other way around. I've learned more about myself from this little boy than I'd care to confess. No, Beau had been right to let me go. I tucked up the blankets to make sure Tommy was covered and left him to his dreams.

The light next to my bed was on, and in the corner was Beau's guitar. To say that my heart was racing was an understatement. I could feel it pound against my chest while my brain screamed, "he's coming."

Only moments before, I was ready to strip down and take him on the couch, and now, I realized I was inadequately prepared for a visit from Beau. When was the last time I shaved my legs? My skin was as dry as jerky, and I couldn't get started on the shortcomings of my body.

I rushed to the window. Yep, it was unlocked. He was coming, but when? Did I have enough time to shower and prepare? What would I wear? My penguin pajamas shouted warm and cozy, not sexy, and certainly not take me. Maybe I'd just climb into bed naked. Would that be too forward?

First things first, I needed a shower and a shave. God help me, and anyone in this house, if I couldn't find a razor.

Stripped to my jiggly bits, I pulled my old, pink bathrobe from the closet and ran to the bathroom. The faucet dripped; the sound created the rhythm I used to prepare myself. I rummaged through the drawers and found an old Schick razor from bygone days and prayed I wouldn't need a tetanus shot when I was finished.

I was in and out of the shower in minutes, no worse for the wear. My hair hung wet and limp over my shoulders. I didn't dare dry it, or I'd wake the house with the roar of what sounded like the outboard motor of a boat.

I debated on makeup, but would I go to bed flexing my full feminine wiles? Was I overthinking this?

I stared down at the jungle between my legs. Holy shit, I'd turned into Sasquatch over the years. I hadn't had a party down there in a long time, so there was no need to trim the lawn. Beau would take one look at me and run.

We didn't even have a decent pair of scissors. All that was in the drawer was a pair of thinning shears, which at this point seemed appropriate. I attacked the forest like a logger in a tree felling championship. It wasn't perfect, but in the end, my thatch couldn't be confused with a wildebeest hiding in tall grass.

When I got back to my room, Beau was on my bed, lying on his side thumbing through the scrapbook I'd dug out from under my mattress.

I closed the door and locked it behind me. "Did you climb up that tree?" I pulled the tie of the robe tighter and gripped the open neck closed.

"Nope, Mr. Peters next door saw me coming and pulled out his ladder."

"Oh, God, you're kidding me?" My stomach turned. The whole neighborhood would know Beau had climbed into my window. I was at risk of dethroning Theresa Platte, the town tramp.

"It would appear the whole town is rooting for us. I have to say, the ladder made it easier to get inside. I didn't have to take that leap of faith and pray that I'd grasp the ledge. I can't tell you how many times I've missed that and landed on my ass."

"But was the jump worth it?"

"Every damn time." He reached out and grabbed the dangling robe tie and pulled me to the bed. "You smell so good." We lay on our sides. The only thing separating us was a tiny bit of fabric and a scrapbook opened to the page that contained our torn picture, and the words that had severed our love.

"Interesting keepsake." The pads of his fingers traced the letters I'd penned.

"It's how an eighteen-year-old girl dealt with grief." I tried to close the book, but he held it open. He lifted his half of the torn picture and repositioned his face to cover the words and bring us back together.

"What are you doing?" I shoved at the book, but it didn't budge. "This isn't important anymore."

"I'm trying to repair the mistake I made years ago." With a gentle caress, he cupped my cheek. "I was an idiot."

My lips gravitated to his palm. "I had an epiphany today." I kissed each of his fingers and pulled his hand to my heart or, more accurately, my left boob.

He pushed the book aside and scooted in, lining up our bodies. "What was your epiphany?" He flexed his palm, filling his hand with terry cloth and titty.

"Leaving me was a good thing."

"What?" He leaned back and rubbed his face. "What do you mean?"

He wasn't following my train of thought. "I sat on Tommy's bed tonight and tried to imagine my life without him, and I couldn't. He's everything good and right in my life. I'm not saying that I was happy you broke up with me, but I experienced things that I might not have ever experienced if I'd stayed or followed you. Who would have thought at nineteen you were so wise?"

"I stalled our life by ten years."

"Maybe, but maybe you gave us time to appreciate each other." I laid my head on his chest and breathed in his scent. He was cedar dipped in sex appeal. "Who knows why things work out the way they do."

He ran his fingers through my damp hair. "I have a ton of regrets, but I won't be making those mistakes again. When my mom said you were back in town, I figured we'd say hi and find some kind of middle ground, but the second I saw you, I knew I'd never leave you again."

"I'm not going to tell you what I thought when I saw you."

"You thought I was an asshole."

Raised up on my elbow, I looked at him lying on my bed just like he had many times before. We'd never made love in my house or his. We'd done a lot of every-thing else, but sex was sacred. We had an unspoken pact that kept us from disrespecting our parents. We'd always gone to the cabin because it was private, and it was our place, but everything had changed. What were the new rules? Were there any?

He rolled to his side and pulled one of my pillows to tuck it under his head. "We need to talk."

CHAPTER SIXTEEN

BEAU

W hen her pinked cheeks faded to white, I knew
I'd chosen the wrong words. "Mandy, I'm not
leaving you."

"It's okay. What do we have in common these days?
I don't know you anymore." She swiped at a tear before
it could fall.

"Stop. You need to let me talk so you don't fill in the
blanks yourself." Her robe fell open, exposing the
creamy skin of her thigh. Distractions were not going to
help me at this moment. Tearing my eyes from her skin
was like pulling a supercharged magnet from metal.
"Would you come to California with me? I want you
and Tommy to come live with me and be mine."

"Wh—what? I thought you were going to—"

"Tell you something you didn't want to hear?" She
dipped her head and pressed it into my chest. "I just told
you that I'm not leaving you—ever."

Her words were muffled against my chest, but I
heard the important ones. "I've heard that before."

"I deserve that, but you know I didn't leave you for me, I left you for you."

She pulled away and played with the buttons on my shirt. "What makes you think we can make a go of it after all these years?"

"We're both single for a reason. You were my one, Mandy, and I won't let you slip away again."

"Oh, I didn't slip, my world tilted, and I tumbled hard into an abyss. Now that you're here, lying under my pink canopy, I feel like my world has been righted, and yet, I don't know how this will ever work. I'm a single mom. I work, and I parent. You perform and travel. I don't have time to be on the road. And what about all those groupies?"

This was a conversation that would require sitting up. Lying down next to Mandy made me want to do everything but talk. I dragged myself into a sitting position and rested my head against the pink padded headboard.

"I'm working on a recording contract with Rocco Piat. It's a three-album deal that will keep me in Los Angeles all the time with the exception of special performances at places like Times Square which I'm doing New Year's Eve. We can put Tommy into a great private school. I have a beautiful house in the hills with views of the Pacific." I tried to keep my voice even, but the pleading tone made its way into my words. *God, she had to say yes.*

"I don't know, Beau, it's a lot to take in." It wasn't the yes I wanted. But it wasn't a no, and that gave me hope.

She straddled my lap and pulled her robe closed, but not before I caught a glimpse of nearly everything. She was killing me one inch of bathrobe at a time. With my hands on her hips, I pulled her close. "Do you love New York too much to leave it?"

Her laughter was pure bliss to hear. "No, it's not that, it's just that I have Tommy to think about."

"But you'll think about it, right?" I watched for any sign of doubt. Her eyes sparkled, her lips quivered at the corners, and her head bobbed like the bobblehead dog my dad had glued to his dashboard.

"Yes," she bubbled. Who knew that joy was palpable, but I could feel it from my heart all the way to my raging hard-on.

"We have to ask Tommy. He'd have to leave his school and his friends. I'm not sure I want to do that to him."

"How about we take Tommy to dinner tomorrow night, and ask him what he wants?"

"What about our date at the cabin?" I loved it when her lower lip jutted out into a pout. I wanted to nip at it and pull it into my mouth, but I knew I'd never stop there. I wanted to hear her scream my name, and there was nothing wrong with Annie Sawyer's ears.

"Oh, we're still having our date. We'll take Tommy to dinner, and then we'll drive by and toss him out the window to our moms."

She gave me a gentle slug to the chest. "That's awful."

"You know I'm crazy about him, but I'm also crazy about you, and I need you like I need air, so I'm pretty sure Tommy will be happy to spend extra time with his grandmas. I'll bribe him with guitar lessons."

"Be careful, he got my mom's genes. He's a charmer and a manipulator. You're going to have to practice the word no."

"For now, all I want to say and hear is yes. By Christmas, you'll say yes to California." I laid her back and covered her body with mine. I'd died and gone to both Heaven and Hell. She was inches from being naked and writhing beneath me. Her hands slid under my shirt and ran up my back. Her movements loosened the tie of her robe, letting it fall open above her waist. "God, you're perfect."

"Hey, mister, these are a D or a C+, at best, barely passing." She pulled the robe closed to hide the plumpness of her breasts.

"These are thesis material, a full report that I intend to study in depth." I pulled her nipple into my mouth.

"Oh, God. It's been way too long." She gripped my head and held me in place. I sucked and pulled at the puckered bud while she lifted her body into mine.

With a pop, I let the nipple go. "How long has it been?" I rose up to see her face.

"Are we going there?" Flushed with the heat of passion, she flopped her head on the pillow and covered her face with her bent arm.

"I think we need to." I rolled to her side.

"Years, that's all you need to know."

Her confession pleased me. "Okay, anything you want to know?"

She lifted onto one elbow and looked around her room. "How many girls?" Her face pinched.

Everything would come out in the end. Wasn't it better to deal with it now rather than save it for later? "Less than you think, and more than I'd like to admit."

She pulled at the lacy comforter, tugging it over her. "Did you love any of them?"

"No, they weren't you." I thumbed her cheekbone. "It was just sex. I promise I never cheated on you. I was never with anyone until after you left for Paris and we weren't talking."

"I wasn't with anyone but Tommy's dad."

That surprised me because Mandy was gorgeous and so damn desirable. "Why?"

"They weren't you." She scooted closer to me. Her citrus shampoo floated through the air. It was the smell of home, happiness, and love. "If I came to California, what would our life look like?"

Passion turned into what if planning. We talked about my house and the neighborhood. "The beach is a short drive and right now the studio is about twenty minutes away, but if I get this deal with Rocco worked out, I'll be working at his studio, which is in Hollywood."

"This is a big deal to you?" The touch of her fingers and the brush of her lips on my chest were pure torture.

"The biggest. It opens up a whole new world for the band. The contract would bring in enough money to set everyone up forever." BT and Bads were rock solid, and all the guys were responsible with their earnings, but a project like this happened once in a lifetime. We weren't

The Eagles or The Stones, but we could very well be in their league once Rocco Piat was finished with us.

"What about work for me?" She shimmied as close as she could. Any closer and she'd be living in my skin.

"You don't have to work."

"But I want to work."

"Whatever makes you happy will make me happy."

"For the first time in a long time, happiness seems possible."

CHAPTER SEVENTEEN

MANDY

I woke up alone. The only clue that Beau had been in my room was the lingering scent of his cologne and the divot in the pillow next to me.

The smell of bacon rose through the floorboards. Mom was cooking.

Once showered, I skipped downstairs and into the kitchen. "Hey."

Mom forked a piece of bacon and pulled it from the pan to the paper towel-covered plate. "Did you two have a nice time?" Her voice was too sweet to be good.

"We talked."

"Is that what they're calling it these days? Is that why old man Peters' ladder is at your window?" Mom carried the plate of bacon to the table and laid out two pieces next to the pancakes she'd put on a plate. "Tommy," she called. "Your breakfast is ready, sweetheart."

"Mom, don't embarrass me in front of my son."

"Oh, honey," she brushed my cheek with her

bandaged hand, "you don't need me for that, you can do that all on your own."

These were the times I wished murder didn't carry such a heavy sentence. "We didn't do anything but talk. Tonight, however, I have a date. Maybe a sleepover, Can you watch Tommy?"

Mom rolled her eyes. "Like you'd have to ask. Should I leave the ladder out or ask Mr. Peters to come and get it?"

Argh. "I'll have Beau take it back. I fell asleep, and I'm sure he didn't want to wake anyone when he left."

"Uh-huh," she hummed in a disbelieving tone.

Tommy traipsed in with his Spiderman backpack overflowing with toys. "Grandma says it's a long drive down the mountain, and I'll need these toys to keep me busy." He grunted as the last Lego was pushed into the tiniest of spaces.

"Good planning. Make sure you behave for everyone. No asking for anything." Tommy didn't have to be reminded. He wasn't that kind of kid. It was probably because he never had to ask for anything. People just gave him stuff all the time.

"He'll be fine." Mom set his plate in front of him. "Eat fast. Grandma Sarah will be here in a few minutes."

I swiped a piece of bacon from the plate and kissed them both. "See you tonight."

Outside, Beau waited with two travel mugs of coffee. "Good morning, beautiful." He rushed over and kissed me senseless.

"I like this service. Coffee, kisses, and a ride. A girl could do worse."

"Baby, you get the coffee and the kisses, but the ride will have to wait for later." His wet tongue slid across his lips and caused desire to heat my blood.

He handed me my coffee and opened my door. Behind him, the ladder sat like a billboard on my front lawn.

The arctic chill had left the air, which meant Sheriff Lerner was right about the storm. As Beau closed the door, I said a silent prayer for our mothers' and Tommy's safety. There was no way they weren't going. My tenacious mother wouldn't let a snowstorm curtail her plans.

I leaned into the dash and looked at the darkening sky. "Looks like a storm is brewing."

Beau's hand covered mine. "They'll be okay. Our moms have been driving in this ever since they traded the horse and buggy for a car."

"Don't let them hear you say that." He was right, I didn't need to worry, but it didn't stop me. That's what mothers did.

"When we get your car back, we'll park it in the garage. You won't need it." He let go of my hand long enough to push the start button.

"Don't you have deals to make, songs to write? I'm expecting a platinum album after this week."

"I'm already working on it. I was thinking about one called 'Grading Scale' or what about 'Blue Balls?'"

"You better not. And if you have blue balls, that's

your fault because I was naked and willing under my robe."

His grumble brought on a laugh. "You're killing me. I'm doing my best to refrain from pulling into the woods and making love to you in the backseat. The one thing saving you is the fact that we have a date tonight."

"What time are you picking me up?" I twisted toward him and took in his profile. Strong jaw. Sun-kissed skin. Sexy as sin eyes. The woods sounded appealing. "I need to know what time I'm getting my cookie."

His lush lips curled into a beautiful smile. "A cookie, huh?"

"Yes, with sprinkles." I pulled the seatbelt as far as it would stretch and whispered in his ear. "Lots of sprinkles."

We arrived at the shop too soon. It had been a long time since I'd been able to make Beau blush all the way to his hairline.

When he opened the car door for me, he didn't let me get far. We staggered toward the wall together with his lips crushed to mine. I tasted his sweetness and a feeling of peace settled over me. This was what we were together. He was chocolate, and I was peppermint, and together we were perfect.

It was a kiss I hoped would last forever, but it turned into something different. A kiss filled with passion turned into a promise. It was a forever kiss, the kind we'd given each other years ago. I fisted his hair and held on tight, so afraid if I let him go, I'd lose him for good.

He pulled away and reached down to adjust his pants. "Guillotine Zipper."

I pressed my head into his chest. "New song title?" With a shift of my hips, I rolled into him and felt just how hard this was for him. "I like it."

"Oh, I'll make sure you like it." He kissed my forehead. "I'll see you at five." He waited for me to get inside before he left. If I knew Beau, he would be spending the day at the cabin making everything perfect.

Inside the shop, I leaned against the door and caught my breath.

"That was some kiss."

I snapped a look at Misty. "How did you know?"

"Peephole." She pointed to the little round disk in the door. I could feel the heat rise to my face. I'd all but climbed the man out in the open for all to see. "So, its back on? Aren't you glad you talked to him?"

I hung my jacket and pulled an apron from the hook. "I'm pleading the fifth."

"Honey, you're guilty. It's written like a confession all over your face. Tell me, how does ten years change a man in the sack?"

There was no way getting past her questions. She stood like a sentry in front of the refrigerator. All ingredients were held hostage until I spilled my secrets.

"I wouldn't know."

"That ladder was under your window for nothing?"

"What? Oh, my God, what's wrong with the people in this town? I need to get back to New York where I'm one in a million and easy to overlook."

"Gossip spreads like wildfire in a small town. Now, give me the dirt."

"We just talked, but tonight, I have different plans." I couldn't stop the excitement that shot through me. Hot, liquid, passion coursed through my veins and only Beau had the power to soothe the burn.

"It's a good thing you're off tomorrow." She stepped aside and let me grab the stuff I needed for today's orders.

"Why's that?"

She patted me on the back in a consoling way. "Has it been that long since you've had a hot, sweaty, sex marathon?" My face must have said it all. "Oh, honey, you're in for a treat."

"Now you're scaring me."

Misty scooped muffin batter and plopped it into paper cups. "If I could be so lucky." She pushed the full tray into the preheated oven. "Hey, I'm kind of sweet on that drummer of his. Can you hook a girl up?"

"Titan? You like Brett Titan?" I couldn't see the attraction myself, but then, I only had eyes for Beau. "He's so inked and grungy and—"

"Sexy?" She grabbed the cookie dough and started scooping it onto prepped trays. "That man makes me wet."

"Oh, don't tell me that." I pulled the muffins Misty had already made from the cooling racks and began to stock the shelves. "Beau asked me to move to California with him."

It took a lot to stop Misty. She was a twirling tornado of energy. Her boobs weren't flat because of her kids.

Her boobs were flat because she lived off a cookie and a gallon of coffee a day, but she stopped dead in her path. "Oh, my God," she squealed. "And?" She bounced on the balls of her feet.

"There's a lot to consider." Indecision coiled inside of me like a spring. I wished the answer could be as easy as saying yes, but it wasn't.

"You have to say yes. If not for you, then say yes for me. I've got vacation in July, and I'm so getting screwed by Brett Titan."

When we opened the doors, the shop smelled of chocolate, and coffee, and possibility. Tonight, I'd lie in Beau's arms. It could be the first day of my forever.

Scott from Alliance brought my keys just before three. A minute later, I raced from the building and straight to my car. It was a short drive, but the snow was coming down hard and fast. The roads were covered and slick all the way home. Once there, I ran into the house and was plummeted straight into Hell.

Water seeping under the door should have been my first clue. Standing in the entry, I watched the water run down the walls.

The pipes must have frozen and burst, and today's higher temperatures had allowed the water to flow freely. Cornflower blue paint peeled from the walls. The sofa my parents picked out years ago was the color of mud instead of sand. Dad's old, wooden radio console and rocking chair sat in two inches of water. The wood had swelled, and the thin layer of laminate peeled like sunburned skin. Not even the record player was spared. A drip from the ceiling splashed across the black vinyl record that had been played just the other night. That particular Bing Crosby album would be forever silenced.

Forced into action, I dashed to the basement and shut off the water to the house. Inches covered the cement floor. Cardboard boxes collapsed around their contents. On my knees, I searched for salvageable items. Everything was soaked. Very little survived. How was I going to explain this to Mom?

With my heart in my throat, I called Beau. As soon as he heard my tears, he told me he was on his way. Everything from walls to carpet would have to be removed and replaced. Both the house and my mom would be gutted.

CHAPTER EIGHTEEN

BEAU

The distress in her voice caused my heart to rattle in its cage. It reminded me of the day I'd told her I wasn't coming back to Bell Mountain. Pure panic pulsed through me. I didn't waste any time. With my keys in my hand, I was in the car before I could say, "I'm on my way."

Hell-bent on rescuing Mandy, I flung the door open without care. My girl was sitting in the center of a soppy room with her head in her hands and sobs racking her body. I slid to my knees in front of her. My blue jeans soaked up the water beneath me. "It's okay, it's just water."

She shook her head. "No, it's more than that. This house is my mom's life."

"No, baby. This house is just where she lives. You and Tommy are her life."

"No, you're wrong." Her breath was choppy. "What am I going to do when she walks in tonight?"

"Hug her. It's not the end of the world." I looked

around the room and wondered if I were right. Annie clung to her past because that's where Mandy's father remained.

"I have to call her and prepare her. She can't walk into this without warning. She can't stay here tonight. It's a mess." She rubbed at her red swollen eyes.

"We have room across the street." I lifted her to her feet and watched as sadness filled her. "I can call her for you?"

She collapsed against my chest. "No, but can you stay while I talk to her?"

"I already told you, I'm never leaving you."

She plucked at the numbers on her cell phone and became as taut as a guitar string the minute her mother answered the phone.

There were no niceties—no happy greetings. No… Mandy approached the conversation like a worn-out doctor. No minced words, just a grim diagnosis. "Mom, I have bad news." This was where the doctor would blurt out, *you have cancer.* Mandy pushed the speaker button.

"Well, I have news, too. We have to stay in Denver tonight. The pass is closed. It's dumped twelve inches in the last four hours. Now, tell me your news?"

Mandy opened her mouth twice but nothing came out. "Mrs. Sawyer, this is Beau. When Mandy came home from the shop she found the pipes had burst, and the ground floor and basement are flooded." The only sound that could be heard was the soaked drywall that drooped and dripped from the ceiling.

"What? But the taps were on? How could that happen?"

"I must have turned them off last night." Mandy's voice cracked as the words spilled from her quivering lips. "I'm so sorry, Mom. It's all gone. Dad's stuff is gone."

"Mrs. Sawyer?" I waited for her to respond. "Mrs. Sawyer," I said again. "I know this is a shock. It's a shock for Mandy, too."

It took a few minutes for her to respond. "Thanks, Beau, Mandy tends to overreact. I'm sure it's not that bad. A little water can be dealt with."

"Mom, it's more than a little water."

"I swear, Mandy, theatrics might have been a wiser career choice. Turn off the water so it doesn't drip all over the carpet and set out a few fans. This happened once before. Call Tippy's and have them come out."

"We'll take care of it. You don't have to worry." There was no use arguing over this with her. Tomorrow would come soon enough. Maybe the storm was a gift, a moment where Mandy and I could be together without any outside influences. And then I thought of Tommy. "Is Tommy okay?"

With the subject changed to Tommy, the conversation became lighter. Annie described their visit to Santa and without telling her what it was, she told Mandy that Tommy had found her a perfect gift. We said hello to the little munchkin and told him to have fun in the hotel. He was super excited about the pool and couldn't wait to hang up.

In the center of the living room, I held my girl. "I

love you, Mandy. This isn't the end of the world. It's a new chapter. Let's call Tippy's and get this under control."

Tippy's Restoration was quick to arrive and assess the damage. They did what they could in the interim, which wasn't much. Old pipes that should have been replaced twenty years ago were the culprits but because Mandy cranked the taps closed last night, she bore the weight of the disaster.

"Let's get your stuff. I have a special evening planned."

She moved like an animal stuck in a tar pit. Once packed, she followed me to the car. This wasn't how I'd pictured our night, but it would seem that nothing with Mandy and me went as planned.

The snow continued to fall, covering the ground like white carpet, creating a fresh slate—a new beginning. When I pulled into the garage, I killed the engine but didn't exit the car.

"Mandy, let it go for tonight. Let's relax and enjoy being together." Worry lines creased her forehead, and I wondered how many kisses it would take to ease them.

She sniffled one last time and pulled her shoulders back. "I need wine and kisses." She didn't wait for me to open her door; she was out of the car and at the entrance in seconds.

"I've got both waiting for you." My lips met hers in a timid kiss. I didn't want to push her when her emotions were so raw. When she pressed her body to mine, I threw caution aside and ravaged her mouth on the threshold of our future. My heart hammered with excitement. Refusing to sever the bond of our lips, I fumbled with the door handle. When it opened, we fell into the cabin —me first, her on top of me, and we stayed there kissing until I heard her stomach protest in a growl. I broke the kiss and traced my fingers over her passion-glazed face until I reached her plump red lips. Soft and gentle—she hovered over me until I was certain my heart would explode. And then I felt it. A quiet calm blanketed me, and I knew I was home. Her lips. Her embrace. Her love. It was the refuge I'd been seeking for years.

"Let me ply you with wine and food."

We climbed to our feet and walked into the kitchen where flowers of every variety sat in vases around the room.

She walked to each vase and touched the delicate petals of the flowers I'd chosen for her. "You didn't need to go to so much trouble." She pulled a daisy from one vase and tucked it behind her ear. "I'm a sure thing, you know."

I poured her a glass of red wine and pressed her against the counter. "You were never a sure thing, Mandy. You were the best thing, and I'd wait forever for you."

"Do you really want to wait?" She shimmied out of her T-shirt and stood in a lacy black bra and her jeans. Skimming her finger under my chin, she pulled me toward the fireplace. "Get the fire going." Her shoes hit the floor one at a time while I fumbled with the matches. After several tries, the kindling I'd set up hours before, ignited. The flame I'd built was small compared to the inferno that blazed inside me.

"Baby, I'll be your fire. Come here."

She stood and slinked toward me like a feline on the prowl. The fire heated my body while Mandy heated my soul. Her hands ran the length of my shirt, gripping the bottom and pulling it over my head. "God, you're sexy." Her voice took on that gravelly quality that made me twitch. "I've missed you for so long." Her hand slid down the front of my jeans, coming to rest on my rock hard length. "So long," she purred as she rubbed my length under her palm.

"Screw finesse. Baby, this is going to be quick, but I promise you the rest of the night. I'll worship every inch of your body, I'll make you forget everything, but right now, I have to have you."

"Take me, Beau." We tugged at each other's jeans until they laid at our feet in a heap. "I love you, Beau."

"Those are the sweetest words I've ever heard." I laid her down in front of the fire and took in every inch of her—ripe and sweet like an apple I wanted to devour.

"And I thought you'd be more interested in the words take me." She shimmied out of her panties and spread her legs.

I couldn't get the damn condom on fast enough. If someone were looking in the window, they would have accused me of being a damn virgin. Once sheathed, I positioned myself between her legs. Her breasts were bountiful and rose to meet my face each time she took a breath.

"These are top of the chart." When my calloused

fingers skimmed her perfect, pink buds, she lifted her hips, and I plunged deep inside her. Damn Heaven. I'd never been anywhere so perfect. My entire body shuddered as I slid in and out of her slick heat.

She whimpered and moaned as I made love to her. I promised fast, but I'd never go before her. A true gentleman always took care of his woman first.

She glistened with arousal, and the minute I massaged her sweet little bundle, she tensed and exploded. Shuddering below my body, she gripped my arms and rode out her orgasm while I searched for mine in the perfect rhythm of her hips. She called out my name just as I found paradise.

Her heart beat in tempo with mine. I was the music and she was the voice. There was no hit song if either element was missing. We were the perfect duet.

Minutes later, I had her soaking in a bubble bath, sipping wine while I prepared her dinner. I was pulling out all the stops to convince her to say yes. My Mandy deserved a perfect life, and I wanted to show her what it would look like with me.

Wrapped in a towel, she walked into the rustic kitchen and picked at the salad on the butcher-block counter. In the oven, cooked the one thing I knew how to prepare. It was a no fuss chicken breast flavored with salt, pepper, and love.

CHAPTER NINETEEN

MANDY

S now the size of cotton balls fell from the cloudy sky,
but I was toasty and warm wrapped in Beau's
arms. We made love all night long, trying to make up for
our years apart. He made me forget everything for a
night, but as the day dawned, so did the realization that
I'd have to face my mom.

"That's hours away. Stop worrying." He pulled me
on top of his body where he convinced me that the
morning was better spent screaming his name.

"What would you think of me adopting Tommy?" His
wet hair dripped on his shoulders. I followed the stream
down his chiseled chest to the towel wrapped around his
waist. Barefoot and almost naked, superstar Beau Tinsel
was making me scrambled eggs and talking about
adopting my son.

Dressed in an old robe I found in the closet, I

hopped up onto the counter and watched him whip the eggs into submission. "Umm...I haven't given it any thought. I haven't even decided to come to California. I haven't traveled anywhere past today in my mind."

"Well, think about it. I'd love to make you both Tinsels."

"Beau Tinsel, if that's a proposal, you're going to have to do better."

"Oh, I'll do better. Right now, I'm planting a seed and hoping it takes root in your heart." I watched the hands that had explored my entire body grip the whisk. I knew the power in his fingers. I knew the softness of his palms.

"My heart seems to be fertile ground for you."

He reached for the salt that sat on the counter and grabbed a handful of my ass in the process. "I can't get enough of you." He poured the salted egg mixture in the frying pan. We watched it bubble and sizzle while he stirred.

"I can cook, you know. I did go to years of culinary school, and I'm pretty sure I mastered scrambled eggs."

He removed the pan from the hot burner and set it aside before he turned to me. Hot hands slid up my bare thighs and slipped under the cotton robe. "This is a selfish endeavor. I want to feed you so I can work you out again." With purpose, he spread my legs and buried his face into the slick heat he created by just existing. "Dessert first." His tongue trailed over my tender flesh, soothing the ache he'd created from hours of lovemaking. His lips were like a magic elixir. Everywhere they touched, I was renewed.

"Oh. Yes." The words escaped without thought as I leaned against the cabinet and let him consume me. Hot tongue. Long strokes. Heavenly sucking. It brought me to that quivering, thigh-shaking place faster than I could have imagined. His wet hair felt good between my fingers as I held on to him and soared. The intensity of my climax, or maybe the unrestrained emotion I felt at being back with Beau, squeezed the air from my lungs. He pulled me to the edge of the counter and slid himself inside of me for a moment.

"Baby, we need to get you on birth control. This feels too good to stop."

I heeled his hips and pulled him back into my warmth. "Don't stop."

"But—" His chest heaved, and his hips shook with each soft stroke.

"I'm on the pill. Have been since Tommy was born. What about you? Do you practice safe sex?" It was a little late to ask now that he was buried balls-deep inside me.

"Always, until now. It's a good thing you're my forever love because you're a bad influence." He ground his hips into me. There was nothing left to come between us. Stroke after stroke, I watched his beautiful face. His jaw clenched with determination while his sapphire eyes looked at me with love. When he called out my name, it was the most beautiful melody; a song I could listen to forever. His head rested on my breasts as he caught his breath. "I love you, Mandy. I always have, and I always will."

Refusing to break our bond, he turned and grabbed

the pan from behind him. On the counter with Beau still buried inside me, he nourished my soul with his words and my body with scrambled eggs.

With our hunger sated for the time being, we showered again and dressed. Mom's morning message said they'd be back at three. Guilt gnawed inside my gut.

I leaned against Beau and watched the snow fall from the trees. The once-heavy branches were now barren, stripped of the snow that clung to them. Tiny rivers flowed into the frozen lake while several fishermen took their chances on the water.

"I'll stay with you and your mom. We can figure it all out together." Beau's love and caring would give me the strength to get through this. However, he didn't need to protect me from my mother. She would pile on the guilt, and then she would take something away from me as punishment. Often, I'd have no clue what that was until it was already gone. It was her way.

"Instead of hanging out with me at Mom's house, can you take Tommy somewhere?" The last thing I needed was for Tommy to get underfoot.

"I'd love to take him somewhere. Did you have a place in mind?"

I had no idea. I was already sifting through wet cardboard boxes and old memories in my mind. "No, just do some boy things. He'd love that, but don't mention California. I want to do that together." I leaned against his body and let out a sigh. Last night was perfect. This morning was perfect. I had a feeling that the afternoon would be everything but.

After a silent goodbye to the cabin, Beau opened the

door and helped me into the passenger seat. His soft kiss fortified me. This afternoon would be a gauntlet of emotions. Mom walked through her life like a wound that hadn't healed—a scab that was constantly being picked—and everything that was destroyed by the water had been her Band-Aid.

Tommy flew out the door as soon as we pulled into the driveway. He was in my arms in seconds. "Mommy, Grandma is crying."

"I know, honey. There was a leak and the water ruined things that Grandma treasured." I set Tommy down and kneeled before him. "Do you remember when Ricky pulled off your stuffed dog's arm?"

"Yes, I was so sad." His little lips curled into a frown.

I cupped his cheek in my hand. "Grandma feels that kind of sad." Beau kneeled beside me and wrapped his arm around my shoulder. "Beau and you are going to hang out this afternoon while I take care of Grandma. Is that okay?"

Tommy's eyes lit up like candles on a cake. "More than okay," he shouted and he was off running toward the house. "I'm getting my coat."

Beau helped me up. "That was a hard sell." Tucked against his chest, I gained the courage to enter the house. "Maybe we should let your mother handle this first part alone."

"I can't. I've abandoned her the last ten years. I can't do it now when she needs me so much." I rubbed my face against his jacket and breathed him in. "I'll miss you."

"I'm just a phone call away. I'll have you back in my arms before you know it."

Tommy ran toward us and managed to stop his forward momentum before he could plow us over. "Are you going to kiss?" He looked up with a toothy grin.

"I think that's a great idea." Beau's lips descended on mine in a sweet, loving kiss. When he pulled away, he looked down at the doe-eyed little boy staring up at him. "Someday, Tommy, you're going to meet a girl who makes you want to kiss her all day long."

"Yuck." He shook his head and scrunched his nose.

"You think that now, but I promise you, son, some girls going to change everything for you."

Beau took Tommy by the hand and led him to the car. I watched them drive away. When the silver SUV shrunk to the size of a pinhead, I pulled myself together and entered the house.

She was sitting in the middle of the living room, sifting through a box of wet photographs. She had pulled plastic bins from the basement and was sorting the salvageable pictures from the complete losses.

"Your dad loved the old Polaroid camera." She handed me a picture that showed Dad and me planting flowers in the boxes out front. That day played clear in my memory. It was close to Mother's Day and it was our surprise for Mom. I was eight and had no idea that I'd never plant flowers with him again. The following winter, he was gone.

"He liked immediate gratification." I tossed the picture into the save box.

"Who doesn't?" Mom pulled the next picture to her

face and brushed it across her lips. When she lowered it, I knew why this was so special. She looked beautiful on her wedding day—beaming from pearl earring to pearl earring. Dad looked damn special in his tux. Their hands were interlaced and it was so easy to see how much they loved each other.

"How did this happen?" She placed the picture in the box and picked up a new stack. That's when I noticed her wrist. It was no longer wrapped in a bandage but was contained in some kind of firm brace.

I reached for her and set my hand on the bone-stiff material. "What did the doctor say?"

"I don't want to talk about it right now." She snuffled and wiped at the tears cascading down her face. "How in the hell did this happen?" Her unsteady voice had raised an octave from start to finish.

Mom didn't normally yell. She was more passive aggressive than angry, but I felt the accusation in her tone. Her words didn't float over me. Each one was like a stinging slap to my face. What she was saying was, *how could you have been so stupid?*

"I'm so sorry, Mom."

"I don't want your sorry. I want to know how I'm supposed to survive everything that's happening?"

Twenty years of this, and I'd just about had it. Over the years, I'd cajoled her and consoled her. My father had died and her heart had shriveled up and atrophied. She'd gone from doting mother to the ice queen overnight.

"Maybe it's time to let some of this go. Maybe it's

time to move forward with your life." I reached for the stack of photos in her hand, but she pulled them away.

"How can you say that to me?" She dropped the photos into the save box, rose to her feet, and squished across the wet carpet. "You have no idea what it's like to lose the one person you love." She pulled ornaments off the tree and put them into a nearby box, oblivious to the fact that her statement cut me deep. "This is my life. It's contained in these pictures, these ornaments, this house." Each word echoed through the air and wrapped around my chest, squeezing hard. That was her problem. She lived through her things, and it wasn't living.

"How dare you tell me I don't know what it's like to lose someone." I stomped to the tree and stood in front of her. "I've lost plenty. I lost Beau for years. But more devastating is the fact that I lost you and Daddy on the same day. I know what it feels like to lose." Filled with rage, I poked my finger at her shoulder. "You gave up. You lost the love of your life and gave up on everything, including me."

"Oh, stop being so melodramatic. I took care of you."

I was angry. I could feel the fury bubbling inside. "You didn't take care of me, you provided for me, but that was it. You shut down, and *I* took care of you. I got you out of bed each morning, I fed you, I cleaned the house." I screamed at her until my throat hurt. "Hell, if we hadn't needed the Sweet Shop to survive, you would have never gone to work. And even then, I worked before and after school to make it all work. I was eight years old, Mom." I pulled over a plastic bin and began to throw the ornaments into it.

"Stop it, Mandy. You're going to break something, and it's all I have."

I pushed past the box of ornaments that sat like an open casket at a wake.

"No, Mom, I was all you had, and you pushed and pushed until you pushed me away." My hurt clawed its way out, and I said the most awful words I'd ever said to my mom. "Maybe Dad didn't jump in to save Beau's dad, maybe he jumped in to get away from you." Body shaking, I rummaged in my bag for the keys to the old Jeep. I left Mom sitting slack-jawed while I ran from the conflict.

The first number I dialed was Beau's, but it went straight to voicemail. I needed him to comfort me, to tell me it would all be all right. Next, I drove to Grady's Diner. I may not get the warm fuzzy from Lou, but she was always good at tough love, and maybe what I needed more than a hug was a swift kick in the pants.

CHAPTER TWENTY

BEAU

Tommy and I stood in the middle of the lake with our lines dropped into the hole I'd cut through the icy surface. Within a few minutes, he had his first tug on the line.

"Beau, it's wiggling." His voice was just above a whisper. I'd told him the fish wouldn't come if he made too much noise.

"Let him get a good bite, buddy. At the next wiggle, I want you to yank your pole back." Determination was etched into his little face. He gripped his pole, the same pole I'd used when I was a kid, and yanked hard. That's when the real fun began.

"Help me. It's so big." He struggled with the reel, so I stood behind him and helped guide in his first catch.

"Fishing is a lot like falling in love." I figured this was the perfect time for guy talk about treating women right. "You never want to raise your voice to a girl, or you might scare her away."

"I don't like girls." He struggled with his pole. "Except for Mommy."

"Someday, a girl is going to turn your head."

"Gretchen did that to me last year and it hurt. My neck ached forever."

I laughed because kids were so literal. "No, Tommy, what I meant is, someday you are going to like a girl, and she is going to take notice of you. So…I want you to talk nice to her. You want to reel her in with your kind words and good deeds."

"Should I feed her worms?" He giggled at his own silliness.

"Yes, but worms for her will be a flower, or a kind word, or sharing your cookie. Then, once you have her on the line, you do nice things for her so you can keep her."

"Do you want to keep my mom?"

"I want to keep both of you."

Tommy dropped the pole and spun around toward me. His quick movements caused me to lose my grip as well. Without any tension, the pole slid into the water and disappeared under the ice cap.

His little hands wrapped like a vine around my waist. "Will you be my daddy?"

"I'd like that, Tommy." I hugged him tight, and I thought about all the days I'd spent on the lake with my father. He'd taught me so much about being a man while we leaned over a gaping hole and pondered fish.

When he turned back to find his pole missing, his eyes bulged like overfilled balloons. "Where did it go?"

"Well, Tommy, that's the next lesson for the day.

When you have something sweet on your hook, you shouldn't abandon it because it could be lost forever." I tugged on the rope I'd tied around his waist for safety. You never knew when you'd run into rotten ice and with the runoff and warm weather today, the lake was unpredictable. I didn't want to feed it. The fishing pole would have to suffice as our sacrifice for the day. When Tommy got older, I'd teach him to use safety picks, but for now, we had tied ourselves to the dock.

While Tommy and I warmed up in the cabin, I checked my phone for messages. It was the second time in as many days I heard Mandy's voice full of emotion. "I'm at Grady's," she whimpered and then she hung up.

"Your mom's at Grady's, are you hungry?" It was getting on dinnertime, and if Tommy was like other boys, he'd be starving.

"Hungry enough to eat the fish I lost." Kids his age hadn't learned how to hide their feelings and a look of disappointment etched his face.

"Buck up, little man. There's always at least one that gets away. But think of it this way, in the spring, someone is going to find a mighty fine fishing pole, so it's like you donated it to a good cause." Of course, I didn't say that the pole would be ruined and most likely attached to a dead fish; those were realities best left for grownups.

Mandy sat in the booth in front of the window, unaware of our arrival. Her cheeks were mottled red and her eyes were puffy.

Lou was at the front door when we arrived.

"Hey, Lou, is she okay?" I glanced toward my seemingly catatonic girl.

"She will be now. Let me take Tommy back to see Rusty. What do you want to eat?" She wrapped her crepey hand around Tommy's.

"You're giving me a choice?"

"We all have choices, Beau, but the bold stand up and voice their desires. Come on, Tommy, Grandpa Rusty has been falling down on the job today. He needs his assistant."

"Hamburger and fries," I called out after her.

"We'll see," she called back before she and Tommy disappeared behind the swinging door.

Mandy's eyes rose to meet mine as I approached. "What's wrong, baby?" I inched in close to her and wrapped her in a hug.

Tears and words flowed from her like a volcano spewing lava. She tore the white napkin into shreds while she told me how the afternoon concluded. When she was finished, I sat in the silence and considered everything. Although my mother was devastated by our loss, she forced herself to push forward for me. Mandy's mom, on the other hand, had done the exact opposite. There were many nights when Mom would send me to fetch Mandy. She'd eat with us and curl up on the couch with Mom until she fell fast asleep. Annie never came looking for her, knowing we'd take care of her. We loved her enough for everyone, and then I'd left her. *Holy shit.* I'd abandoned her just like her mom.

As a testament to the goodness within, she sat beside me, more worried about her mom than anything else.

"I'll text my mom and ask her to look in on yours."
It was seconds after I pressed send that Mom replied.

She's here. Maybe you should stay at the cabin with Tommy and Mandy. Annie is dealing with a lot right now.

Mandy leaned on me, but I was happy to take on whatever weight she needed me to carry. So many people had depended on her for everything. It was time for that to change.

Tommy and Lou came out of the kitchen bearing gifts. Tommy held the hamburger and fries I thought were mine. When I reached for the plate, he shook his head. "This is mine. Grandma Lou has yours." He flopped onto the bench and dug into his fries.

Lou set a cup of soup in front of Mandy and a plate full of meatloaf and mashed potatoes in front of me. "Hey, where's my hamburger?" I plucked a fry from Tommy's plate and popped it into my mouth.

Lou narrowed her eyes at me. "Your request lacked enthusiasm." She ruffled Tommy's hair and walked back to the kitchen.

Mandy sat and stared at the soup. She made no effort to eat, so I spoon-fed her. "Open up." I placed a spoonful of the chicken noodle soup in her mouth and turned my attention toward Tommy while she swallowed.

"How about we have a sleepover at the cabin? The Grandmas are having a sleepover, so why shouldn't we."

Tommy's expression brightened. "Can we tell spooky stories?"

"I'm not sure about that, but we can toast marsh-mallows at the fire pit."

I spooned another bite into Mandy's mouth, hoping that once she was fed, she'd engage with us.

"S'mores? Maybe we can find my fishing pole."

That got her attention. She sat up straight and pulled the spoon from my hand. "What fishing pole?"

"Daddy Beau and I went ice fishing." He sat tall and proud. "The fish tugged too hard and pulled it under."

Eyes full of accusation turned my way. "You did what?" She slapped the table, causing her torn confetti to take flight.

I waited for the last piece to settle before I explained. "You said to do boy things, and I thought about my best memories with my dad, and they were always on that lake."

"How could you? You know what happened on that lake." She pushed the soup from in front of her. The warm liquid splashed over the side.

"He was safe, Mandy. We went over every safety precaution. He's a smart kid."

She turned on me like a rabid dog. "Yes, but he's not your kid."

Tommy chimed in. "Yes, I am, Mommy, Beau is going to be my daddy."

Her blotchy complexion turned red. "You told him that? I asked you not to say anything to him."

Tommy's head bobbed left and right while his mother and I argued. "I didn't. He asked if I would be his Daddy, and I told him I'd like that very much."

"You don't get to make those choices." Every eye in the diner was on us.

"I thought we were past this, Mandy. I thought we were together."

"Argh," she groaned. "Let me out." She shoved at my body, forcing me to stand up. "Let's go, Tommy." She held out her hand, but he didn't take it.

"No, Mommy, I have choices too, and I want to stay and eat, and then go to the cabin and make S'mores."

"Tommy, this isn't the time to be difficult. Let's go." Mandy stomped her foot once and stared at her son.

"Let him eat. I'll bring him to the cabin. He's safe with me, Mandy." I pulled the key to the cabin off the ring and handed it to her. "You go ahead. We'll be there in a while. You and I need to talk about this," I looked around at the people who had lost interest in our conversation and had gone back to eating, "but this isn't the place."

She swiped the key from my fingers and leaned over to kiss Tommy. "Be good. Mommy will see you in a little while."

She stood back and stared at me as if deciding to trust me or not. In the end, she chose in my favor because she turned around and walked out of the diner.

"Did you tug too hard?" Tommy talked over a mouthful of fries but I understood his meaning.

"I hope not, buddy."

CHAPTER TWENTY-ONE

MANDY

W hat the hell was I thinking? What the hell was he thinking? I tottered between regret and rage. I knew he was trying to help, but why the lake? Every bad thing that ever happened was because of that damn lake.

I felt the lie as soon as I gave it life. Not everything bad happened at that lake. It was where I first made love to Beau. It was where I went when I needed a quiet place to contemplate. It was where he'd filled my body and heart with his love.

No, the lake wasn't bad. I'd made it the villain when, in reality, it was Mom and me who had let it continue to suck us into its cold, vacant depths. She'd drowned while I'd run as far away as I could.

The first thing I did when I arrived at the cabin was walk onto the dock. Two ropes were tied to the pylons, proof that Beau was looking out for my boy. I sat on the edge and looked to the place that had swallowed my father. He was gone, but I still felt his presence in this place he loved so much.

I'll never forget the first day he took me fishing. It was spring and we had rowed to his favorite spot, dead center in the water. We pulled in our bag limit and sat sipping soda. "Respect nature, Mandy," he'd said. "It will always give you what you need, but if you're not careful, it can take it all back."

Dad had to know the ice was thin that day, but he must have thought the risk was worth the reward. I knew in my heart if he had to do it all over again, he'd have done it another way.

The sun had set, taking with it the warmth that had soaked into my skin. Headlights lit up the dock like a runway. I walked toward Beau and Tommy, who exited the car with grocery bags and smiles.

"Mommy, we got everything for S'mores." How could I not get excited about S'mores when Tommy was so exuberant? Honestly, it was all kinds of goodness wrapped into one melted, mouthful of joy.

I grabbed the bag from Tommy. "How about I prep the goodies while you men build the fire?"

Beau didn't say a word, but he walked to me and pressed a gentle kiss to my lips. "I brought you a surprise."

With the bag in between us, I fell into his chest, crushing its contents. "I'm sorry, Beau. You are so good, and I don't deserve you."

He chuckled, "No, you deserve better than me, but you'll have to live with the disappointment." One more quick peck on my lips, and he was off gathering wood.

I rushed into the cabin to put the components on a tray. First went the marshmallows, then the chocolate bars, and finally, the graham crackers. Chocolate kisses and peppermint candies were the last items I removed from the bag. Beau was looking for something special tonight. I popped a peppermint into my mouth and rushed outside. I had a sweet little boy and a sexy hot musician waiting for me.

Tommy tittered on about the fish he was certain was forty inches long. I stared into the fire, trying to figure out how I'd make things right with my mom. She wasn't completely at fault. She'd bailed on me the first ten years, and I'd bailed on her the last. I'd say we were about even. In the future, I'd have to make coming home a priority. Seeing Mom once a year in New York wasn't going to mend the fences we'd erected around our hearts. I needed her, and she needed me. We'd figure it out.

Beau's ringing phone silenced everything. "Hello? Oh, hey, Brent, did you get me what I wanted?"

Tommy and I chowed down on S'mores while Beau talked. "What do you mean no?"

Uh oh, this didn't sound good at all. I tapped Tommy's arm to get his attention and pointed toward the dock, but Beau shook his head and signaled for us to stay.

"It's three days before Christmas, and he can't wait?" His jaw muscles flexed and tightened. "Hold on."

Beau covered the receiver with his hand. "It's my agent. I've been trying to reschedule this meeting with Rocco for after Christmas, but he insists we meet tomorrow. I can fly out tomorrow morning and be back tomorrow night."

My heart ached with the knowledge he'd be leaving me again, and he must have seen it on my face.

"I'm coming back, Mandy."

I knew I was being silly. Hadn't he told me about this opportunity just days before? It was the biggest deal of his career. How could I deny him?

"I know, you should go, you need to go."

He beamed me a bright smile then uncovered his phone and pulled it to his ear. "I'll be there tomorrow at noon. You have tomorrow to close this deal, Brent because I want to be with my family." His meaning was clear when he said the word family, his love for Tommy and me was written all over his face.

With Tommy tucked into bed, I found Beau at the kitchen table looking over the contract Brent had emailed him. It was easy to wrap my arms around his neck, easier to nibble at his neck, but what was hard to take in were the zeroes in his contract. "Is that millions?"

He tugged me close enough to kiss me. Yep, he was chocolate, and I had eaten a peppermint.

"Perfect." He licked his lips and spun me around to sit on his lap.

"No...really...is that millions? Is that for the whole band?"

Wood on wood was never a great sound, but I barely

paid attention to the screech when Beau slid his chair out and turned me to straddle him.

"Yes, it's millions and no, it's our share."

"Ours?"

"Baby, what do think us being together means?"

"Oh, Beau, I don't want your money. I'm just flabbergasted you make so much." His scruff felt divine against my face. Yep, all I needed was him.

"I generally give half to charity. Soup kitchens have received the bulk of my donations in the past. Every check I wrote made me feel closer to you." His hands gripped my ass and pulled me tight against him.

"I love that you give as much as you get. You've always been generous to a fault." Generous enough to give me the freedom to find myself, but I was nothing without him.

"Shall we go to bed so I can give you more?"

I hopped off his lap and started toward the bedroom. "Race you."

Despite my head start, he made it to the bed before me, but I was naked before him. By the look in his eyes, he was going to be downright philanthropic tonight.

"Mandy, I've got to go." His lips hovered over mine. "I have just enough time to get down the mountain and catch my plane. I'll be home tonight." He brushed at my lips. "There's money on the counter, maybe you and Tommy can get a new tree and put it up here. Wouldn't it be nice to bring in our first Christmas together?" His hand slipped under the T-shirt I wore and cupped my breast. "I want to kill my agent right now. I want you so damn bad."

"I want you, too, but you have to go, and I have to be at the shop. It's come to work with Mommy day."

Beau kissed me once more before he left. The minute I heard his car rumble to life, I felt empty inside. However, I didn't have time to let the feeling soak in and take over. Tommy and I had a lot to take care of today.

He was sitting at the table with a bowl of Chex and glass of juice. "Did you get that yourself?" I squeezed behind him and scooted into the corner chair by the window.

"No, Daddy Beau got it for me." My heart lurched. "He also made you coffee." Tommy tilted his head toward the counter where a cup was waiting for me. "I think he's trying to reel you in, Mommy. You're the fish he's trying to catch."

It had been a long time since I'd snorted when I laughed. Damn good thing I didn't have a mouthful of coffee, or I would have spit it everywhere.

"How do you think he's doing?"

"How am I supposed to know, I'm only six?"

For a six-year-old, he understood far too much. "We have to go to the shop and then to see Grandma. Let's get shaking."

Fifteen minutes later, we were on our way. When we got to the shop, Misty was on full-tilt. We had a large cookie order that no one bothered to mention, and she was racing around the backroom like a headless chicken. The one benefit to being so busy was I didn't have time to worry about anything but cookies. Tommy sat in the corner, colored, and ate far too many sweets. I'd called in backup help that would arrive around noon. They might be teenagers, but they were going to earn their pay.

Lola and Sam arrived at noon. I put them to work icing the wreaths. If my young son could ice a cookie, so could a kid three times his age. It turned out, they couldn't. Two dozen cookies had to be rescued before I assigned one of the girls dishes and the other the register. My mother was right. No one could run this shop better than a Sawyer. Mom had to get right as rain soon. The shop wouldn't survive long-term without her.

Once everything was under control, Tommy and I headed home. A big Tippy's Restoration truck was outside, along with an industrial size dumpster. My hopes didn't soar because I knew nothing but carpet and sheetrock would go into that bin. Mom would hang on to everything else like it was a lifeline.

"Mom?" I tiptoed in and peeked around the corner, two men were sweeping up what was left. All that remained in the living room was two by four walls, a water-stained subfloor, and dangling overhead lights. I found Mom putting fresh grounds in the old percolator. "Mom?" I repeated. She cocked her head my way. She'd aged a decade overnight. "I'm so sorry." I ran to her and hugged her with all my might. She was my mother, and despite her being her, I loved her.

"Where's Tommy?" Of course, she would ruin my warm gooey feeling of affection by not acknowledging my apology.

"He's upstairs packing his bag. We're staying at the cabin."

Mom pulled two cups from the cupboard and set them on the counter before she shuffled to her seat. The kitchen had escaped ruin, as did the upstairs. The major fatalities involved the living room, the staircase, and the basement, which housed Mom's treasures.

"We have to talk, Mom." The chair scraped across the checkered floor. When I looked down, I groaned. This was the chair with the cracked vinyl that managed to pinch my ass each time I sat. I half-cheeked it and tottered on the edge.

"You're right, we have to talk." She rearranged the salt and pepper shakers, rotating the salt to the right, and then to the left, and back again.

"What I said yesterday was wrong, and I feel guilty for being so mean."

She patted my hand with her good hand. "It wasn't one of our finer days, but I learned a bit yesterday, too. I also got a crash course in Sarah Tinsel's don't be an ass class."

I ribboned my fingers through hers. "Oh yeah, what did that look like?"

"Mostly it was her mouth moving constantly. All I heard her say was that I'd been an absentee mom, and I'd been drowning myself in sorrow for way too long. It was time to move forward."

Without thought, I nodded my head in agreement. It was time to move forward. I was traveling in that direction with Beau, and I prayed Mom would work her way ahead as well.

"You weren't a terrible mom. You were just…" There were no nice words for unavailable or disconnected. So, I went with the adage, *if you can't say something nice…*

"I'm going to work on it, but I need something from you." Her eyes filled with a look of hope I hadn't seen in years.

"Anything, Mom. I'll do anything." And I meant it. Whatever it took, I'd do it. "Tell me what you need."

Mom stood and walked to the old coffee pot. A wisp of steam rose from the two cups she poured. "The Sweet Shop has been in our family for decades. Daddy and I bought the building from your grandfather when we got married."

Preparing for a trip down memory lane, I made myself comfortable by sliding onto the chair. The familiar pinch of the plastic terrorized my tush. Replacing these chairs would be a priority during Mom's forward momentum. "Why do you think Daddy decided on opening a bakery and candy shop as opposed to a hardware store or a music store? It's not like he had a background in sweets." I'd always wondered how we became known for confections.

"He did it for me. I loved to bake, and the town didn't have a place where young and old could gather and enjoy each other." Mom opened the kitchen drawer and pulled out an envelope. It took her two trips to return to the table. When she did, she plopped in her favorite chair. It gave her a panoramic view of the kitchen from the Bing cherry wallpaper to the Chubby

Checker records. "He did it for you. He wanted a Sawyer to run it for generations to come."

"I bet he's smiling down from Heaven. You've done a good job."

Mom held onto the envelope like it was her salvation…or her death sentence—her grip so tight her knuckles turned white. Whatever it contained would change my life, this I knew in my gut.

"I've lost everything in the house except for a few boxes of pictures." The blood flowed back into her hands the minute she set the envelope in front of me. "And now it's time for me to step aside and let the next generation take over."

I caressed the envelope with shaking fingers, hoping my light touch would soften the blow inside.

"Mom, whatever it is, we'll attack it together. Whatever you need, I'll be here." I had no idea what the paper I pulled from the envelope was, it wasn't a deed. It was a diagram of a wrist. Words like sensory neuropathy, irreversible, and chronic jumped from the page. "What does this mean?"

"It means my wrist will never get better. I'll never be able to scoop muffins, or stir batter, or pipe icing with my good hand again." Tears rolled down her face and dripped to the table. "It means I need you to come home for good. I'll lose the shop without you, and you know I can't lose the shop."

Thank God the crack in the vinyl had gripped my ass, or I might have fallen out of the chair. What the hell was I going to do? My dream of ocean views and long, loving nights with Beau evaporated.

"Mom, I can't."

"You have to Mandy. If not for me, do it for Dad. Don't let his dream die."

"You don't know what you're asking me to do. What you're asking me to give up."

"I'm asking you to come home so we can be a family again. I'm asking for you to give me a chance to make it all right. I'm asking for an opportunity to be not who I was, but who you wanted me to be. Selfless should have been your middle name."

No words came to me. If I stayed, I knew I'd say all the wrong things, so I ran.

Tommy tried to keep up with me as I dashed from the house. "Mommy, you're going too fast." His steps were two to my one. He was the kite, and I was the string pulling him toward the car.

"I'm sorry." I slowed to a quick walk. With a glance over my shoulder, I half-expected to see my mother race from the house to stop us, but she didn't. No, she was still sitting at the table sipping her coffee and timing my return.

She hadn't learned that I was good at avoidance. It was a skill that took me years to master. Avoidance was another word for abandonment. The same thing I'd accused her of and here I was, equally guilty. I'd left her years ago when my heart stopped beating. I'd left her alone to survive, knowing full well she wasn't capable.

Twenty minutes later, Tommy and I were tucked into the cabin. Tommy went straight for the television while I took a seat at the table. Just this morning, I looked over Beau's shoulder at the contract that would change his life. My eyes closed, and I pictured the doctor's report that would change mine.

"Damn it." Flat-palmed, I pounded the table.

"You okay, Mommy?" Tommy pulled his eyes from the cartoon to look at me.

"Yes, sweetie. I'm good." Lies were never my thing, but what purpose would it serve to tell my little boy that in the next few hours, I'd make a decision that would forever change our lives.

CHAPTER TWENTY-TWO

BEAU

Today was a day to celebrate. I signed a three-record deal with Rocco Piat that would change the lives of many people, but each time I called Mandy, her phone went straight to voicemail and my excitement lessened when I couldn't share it with my love.

When I talked to my mom, she said she hadn't talked to Annie or Mandy all day. They must be finished exorcising the house by now. It was eight o'clock and I was still at the airport, trying to get a flight.

On a last-ditch effort, I dialed Mandy again.

"Hello." Her shrunken voice was a whisper.

"Mandy, I was worried."

"I'm good." Short and succinct weren't her style. Something was wrong.

"You're not good."

A long pause. "You're right." Her voice trembled, and I waited, but she didn't elaborate.

When had this wall gone up between us? And how was I going to get past it? "What's wrong, baby?"

182

"Don't call me that."

"What in the hell is happening?" The air around me was heavy and thick with dread. I could sense her slipping away, that wall growing higher and thicker with every second. "I'm stuck here tonight, but I'm catching the first plane out tomorrow."

"No. You need to stay in Los Angeles. You need to stay away from me." Her words were flat and fast. Firm.

"No, baby. You and Tommy are coming to Los Angeles so we can be a family." My lungs withered, my heart curled in like a fist. "Mandy, let me—"

"I get to choose, not you, and I don't choose you." A half a sob, then she hung up. All that remained was silence.

After a dozen calls, I gave up and called the airline on a last ditch effort. There were no charter flights available and no earlier flights before my scheduled afternoon flight tomorrow. Everyone seemed to be traveling for the holiday. Feeling defeated, I called Mom.

"Hey, sweetie. It's late." Her noisy television muted. "Everything okay?"

"No. Something is wrong. What in the hell is going on there?" I'd never considered what desperation sounded like, but it felt horrific. Mandy had reached down my throat and yanked my heart out one blood vessel at a time.

"I don't know, Mandy ran from the house this afternoon. I guess her mom told her the news."

"What news?"

"Annie's injury is permanent."

"Are you sure?" That was terrible news, but it wasn't

a reason to throw what we had away. "What does that mean?"

"Yes, I'm sure. She talked to several specialists. She has little to no feeling in her hand which means she can't work. I'm sorry I didn't say anything, but it wasn't my story to tell." I couldn't fault my mom, she'd never told Mandy why I let her go years ago. It wasn't her place. Mom excelled at confidentiality.

"Mandy broke up with me, Mom?"

"She what?" Mom inhaled and exhaled several times.

"She told me I wasn't her choice."

"Oh, Beau, she's not being honest with herself. When it comes to you, she has no other choice."

"She made some other choice today. One that didn't include me."

"Did you sign that contract that would keep you in Los Angeles for the next three years?" There was something telling about Mom's tone. It was a crumb, maybe a missing piece to a puzzle.

"Yes, I've never seen anything like it. What an amazing experience. The contract was so detailed, it took hours to go over. It's why I missed my plane tonight. Now I'm back home, hoping the travel agent can find me a flight. I need to get back to Mandy and figure this out."

"Honey, Mandy let you go because she loves you. She's staying in Bell Mountain to take over the Sweet Shop."

An Einstein I wasn't, but I got my answer. She was making a choice for me. She was repeating the mistake

I'd made years ago. Relocating to Los Angeles would take her a thousand miles from her mother. Not far enough in normal circumstances, but these weren't normal times. Mandy's mom had lost twice this week— bad news about her wrist and a devastating flood. Mandy was honoring her family by giving me up.

I brewed a cup of coffee and stared at the ocean from my living room window. The contract I'd signed today had sealed our future. Unless I was willing to bankrupt everyone in the band, I would lose Mandy. Choices were a funny thing. They were given and taken away without impunity.

Yesterday, it looked like the world was our oyster; today, we were stuck with the shell.

CHAPTER TWENTY-THREE

MANDY

My heart lodged in my throat as I prepared to exit Beau's cabin for the last time. Overwhelmed with joyful memories, I walked through the rooms and whispered goodbye to happiness.

My fingers gripped the note I'd written—a few words that couldn't begin to convey what I was feeling.

Beau,

I'm so sorry.

I'll always love you.

Mandy

Set on his pillow, I left it in hopes that someday he'd find it, and hate me less.

Tommy tugged at my hand. "Mommy, why are you sad?"

"I'm okay, buddy." And I would be because Tommy needed me to be. "Shall we go to the shop?"

"When is Beau coming home?"

Talk about an aching heart. Mine was sixty percent destroyed but the forty percent left behind screamed in agony. Swallowing the lump in my throat, I picked up my little man and hugged him. Family was my priority.

"He has some business in California. I'm not sure when he's coming back."

"But he has to, Mommy. Beau is going to be my daddy." Tears caught in the corners of his eyes. He wouldn't understand why we had to let Beau go. All he understood was that something wonderful had disappeared.

"Ah, sweetie. Beau will always be your friend." I prayed that was true.

"Doesn't he love us anymore?" Tommy wiggled from my arms and landed on his feet. "Why is he in Los Angeles when we aren't there?"

"I asked him to stay and follow his dream, Tommy. Beau's band has a big opportunity, and he can't do what he needs to do if he stays with us."

He swept his sorrow from his eyes and sniffled. "We can go to him."

"No, buddy, we can't. Grandma needs us to stay here and help her." It was time to break the news. "We're going to stay in Bell Mountain. Grandma is going to take care of you while I run the Sweet Shop."

His expression was a cross between delight and bewilderment. "We are going to live with Grandma?"

"For a while, but we'll find our own place soon."

"Can we stay at the cabin?" Tommy looked around the living room. He'd settled in here like it was his home.

"No. We can't. Beau's not too happy with me right now."

Arms across his chest, he stomped his foot. "I'm not happy with you right now."

"Stand in line, buddy." With his backpack in my hand, I led my son into our uncertain future.

"What do you mean you broke up with Beau?" Misty dumped dark chocolate chips into the mixer and set the paddle to low.

"It was for the best. We're different."

She furrowed her brow. "Bad in the sack, eh?"

"God no, that was amazing—a rock-star performance."

"You're a damn lunatic." She tested the dough and nodded her head. "This guy loves you, he's good in bed, and he's rich. You're throwing away a damn trifecta. What the hell is wrong with you?" Her agitation showed in the way she manhandled the mixing stand. It was industrial strength and weighed hundreds of pounds, but when she pulled the bowl free, she sent the stand wobbling. "This is about your mother, right?"

I chewed on my cheek and her question. "Isn't it always about my mother?"

"I knew it." She pulled the cranberry orange muffins from the oven while I dipped candy canes in chocolate. Each one was a reminder of the kisses I'd no longer receive.

"She needs me. Her wrist will never heal, and you can't run the shop by yourself. After working with those teens, it's obvious you need experienced help."

Misty growled like an angry animal. "I refuse to be a part of this. If you want to be a martyr, have at it, but don't use me as your excuse." She stomped around the shop, banging trays and throwing utensils. "The employment pool is lacking here, but I could have made do."

"This isn't about you." Agitation vibrated in my chest. "This is about honoring my family. Making sure my mom doesn't lose everything she holds dear. It's about leaving a legacy for my son. Remembering my father's sacrifices. I can't throw that away."

"I always liked you, Mandy, but not today. Today, I'm so mad at you I could spit tacks. Family isn't defined by who's in your past. It's who's in your future that counts too, and now yours is looking as barren as mine."

I was zero for two today. When I'd dropped Tommy off at Mom's, he didn't even say goodbye. He stomped into the house and fell into her arms and cried.

We opened the doors to let in the old duffers. Christmas music floated through the speakers, but I felt anything but joyful.

All day long, I watched the door with expectation. Would Beau show up? Did he catch that next flight like he said he would? Each bell brought the height of anticipation and the weight of despair. Beau was nowhere to be seen.

Theresa bounced in near closing time. She flashed her phone my way and showed me a picture of Beau at lunch with his agent and his niece. I knew there wasn't anything going on between them, but it still hurt to see them sitting together with smiles on their faces while I drowned in self-inflicted despair. "Sorry it didn't work out with you and Beau?"

I wanted to yell at the unfairness of the world, but I'd made the choice. I'd set Beau free so he could get what he'd always dreamed of. In twenty years, when they were inducting him into the Rock and Roll Hall of Fame, I'd sit back and smile knowing that without my sacrifice, he might not have made it. Beau Tinsel was big lights and bright cities. He was screaming fans and autographs. He wasn't Bell Mountain.

"You win some, you lose some." I bagged the remainder of the goodies we had left and handed them to Theresa. She wasn't a bad person. She had just never experienced the love of a man like Beau. His smile could brighten my cloudy day. His hug could wrap me in happiness, and his kiss would imprint on my heart forever. I was a better person because of him and because I'd been a recipient of his love. How many women would never have a Beau moment? "Here, take these with you. We all deserve a little sweet in our lives."

Her over-sprayed hair stayed in place as her head tilted to the side. "I wish it could have been different for you." Sincerity warmed her otherwise cool voice. Despite her fake nails, artificially plumped lips, and hair dye, something real shined forth from Theresa Platte that I'd never seen before—compassion. "If the fairytale can't come true for Bell Mountain's sweethearts, then we're all screwed." She gripped the bag, turned in her boots, and walked out the door.

"I'm still mad at you," Misty called from the back room, "but that was nice." We were closing early today for the holiday. The shop would be closed until New Year. It was the slowest week of the season with everyone sugared out from Christmas. It would give me time to go back to New York and prepare for our move.

"I can get the rest." I took the tray from her hand and walked her to her door. "My mom has Tommy, and you should be with your family. I hope you get what you want for Christmas."

She rolled her eyes like a kid. "You already screwed that up. How am I supposed to get Brett Titan without you?" She pulled me in for a hug. "You screwed us up. I had me with Brett, Theresa with Tate Ripley, and I was figuring out the rest. Sheesh." She pulled off her apron and tossed it on the stainless steel prep table. "Get home to your boy."

It took thirty minutes to finish cleaning up. When I turned off the lights and music, I received a glimpse into my future. It would be as grim and dark as the shop was at the moment. There would be no more music. No more bright laughter. That was the past.

With the house flooded, and the tree stripped bare, the least I could do was pick up a few extra gifts for Tommy. After leaving Bobo's Toyshop with a few extras I knew Tommy would love, I drove at a snail's pace home. This was going to be an interesting Christmas, and I wasn't in a hurry for it to arrive.

What greeted me when I walked into Mom's house was a surprise. The carpet and soggy furniture were gone. Garland and lights hung from the two by four walls. Beanbag chairs were strewn about the freshly laid plywood floor. In front of the window sat our naked tree; boxes of ornaments surrounded it.

"What do we have here?"

"Grandma says we have to savage the holiday."

"It's salvage, honey." I kneeled in front of Tommy and kissed his nose. "It means to save, and it's a great idea." The smell of dark chocolate filled the air. "What's Grandma making?"

"We're making brownies. She put in the ingredients and I stirred. You're right, Mommy, her hand doesn't work so well. She tried to stir, but the bowl crashed to the floor, and we had to start over again. She said she has to stick to soft stuff like pancakes."

Even though the choice I'd made was hard, deep inside I knew it was the best decision. Tommy would get to know his grandmother. He'd grow up in a place where everyone would know him and love him. He'd never get that in New York or California. Here, he'd be one of the few, not one of the many.

"Mandy." Mom walked in carrying a tray of brownies. "I'm so glad you're home." She looked around the room and shrugged. "We did a little redecorating today. What do you think?"

With my hands on my hips, I traipsed through the colorful bags—four in all. "Are we expecting company?"

"Grandma Sarah is bringing pizza. She's going to help us decorate the tree."

"Nice." It was the one word I could muster. I loved Beau's mom like she were my own, but how would it be now that I'd left him?

"Get the music, Tommy." Mom placed the brownies

in the center of the floor. Her once put-together living room resembled a hostel.

Tommy ran out of the kitchen with an iPod. "Where did you get that?"

"Sarah had an extra one she lent me until I can get one for myself. Thank goodness for Tommy, otherwise, I wouldn't have been able to fill it with the music I love." She pushed a button and good old Bing sang about a white Christmas.

Mom looked toward where the old record players used to sit.

"What did you do with everything?"

"I got rid of it. You were right, Mandy, I was living in the past. I wasted so many of your years holding you there with me. I'm sorry." She brushed her tears away with her hand brace. "Lots of things are going to change." She ruffled Tommy's hair. "Isn't that right, Tommy?"

"Do you think it was wise to let a six-year-old decorate your living room?"

"Why not, it turns out he has pretty good taste." She flopped down onto the purple beanbag. Tucked beside it was an old Polaroid camera. "While you two decorate, I'm going to collect new memories." She snapped the first shot of me with my mouth hanging open.

"Who stole my mother?"

Tommy was already at the tree hanging the ornaments we'd hung a week ago. He attacked it with the kind of passion only a kid could harness.

Before she could answer, Sarah walked in with

several boxes of pizza. She looked at me and smiled. "Merry Christmas, Mandy."

Heavy-hearted, I walked to her and took the boxes from her hands. "Merry Christmas, Sarah."

She shook her head at me. "Why start with formalities now? You've always called me Mom."

"I know, but that was…"

"Just yesterday. Not much has changed." She kissed me and pulled me, boxes and all, in for a hug. "It will be okay, Mandy."

I was grateful for her understanding. Because of me, she wouldn't have her son home for Christmas.

"Come sit down, Tommy, it's time for dinner."

After pizza, we gorged on brownies and decorated the Christmas tree. Mom disappeared into the kitchen and came back with a package of silver tinsel. Tommy loved tinsel, as was proven by his shout of glee. It didn't take him long to open the box and toss it in the air like last time. The strands fell like icicles over the tree. When he turned around, the back of his head was silver.

"Come here," I said. "Let me pull those off you. The trouble with tinsel is that it shows up in places you least expect." I pulled the strands from his dark hair and hung them from the tree.

Sarah and my mother exchanged looks. Those two were always up to something. "What are you up to now?"

They both pasted on shocked expressions. "Nothing. We're just happy Tommy is going to have a Christmas after all. It wasn't looking too promising there for a while."

They were right. Tommy was going to have his first family Christmas. This was how it would be for many years—Mom, Tommy, and me. It wasn't how I pictured my life, but it wasn't bad. I could be miserable and all alone. Instead, I was miserable and lonely and that wouldn't do.

Mom had drowned herself in sadness, and it had made a profound impact on my life and even the life of my son. This was a new beginning, and I'd attack it like an ant on a sugar hill.

"Tommy?" He was mid-bite into his third brownie. Soon, he'd suffer a sugar crash and be fast asleep. "Finish up your brownie. Santa won't come if you're awake."

He shoved the rest in his mouth. Chipmunk-cheeked, he rounded the room and kissed the Grand-mas. "I miss Beau," he mumbled.

"He's in California, taking care of business. If he could be here, he would be." Sarah hugged Tommy tight, and my heart fell to my stomach. I missed Beau, too. I always would. He'd be my forever love.

After Tommy was asleep, Sarah, Mom, and I brought out the presents we'd been hiding in closets and under beds. I was so grateful that Mom kept her rule of no presents under the tree until late Christmas Eve. Her rigid rule saved the day.

Exhausted from an emotional day. I entered my room. In the corner, sat Beau's guitar. My heart thundered at what it used to mean. It no longer announced his visit but was a stark reminder of his absence.

CHAPTER TWENTY-FOUR

MANDY

The day began with a shout of excitement and little feet padding into my room.

"Get up, Mommy, Santa has come." He tossed me the old bathrobe and tugged at my arm. "Let's go. Let's go."

His joy was contagious. How could I not smile when his grin was taking up his face? "I'm coming." I pushed my hair from my face and sat on the edge of the bed. One glance at the guitar in the corner sent me on my way. Tommy flew down the stairs while I gripped the banister and took them one at a time. Without my first cup of coffee, nothing moved fast. It was the kick-starter to my day, and without it, I could barely turn over my engine.

Mom came to the rescue with a mug of coffee and a plate of sweet rolls and croissants. "Sarah is on her way. She wants to see Tommy open his gifts."

"Aww," Tommy groaned. He already had one in his lap and had torn the paper a bit.

"You can wait a minute. No one is taking your presents away." I sipped at the elixir of life found in a ceramic mug.

Nestled in near the tree, I looked out the window toward the Tinsel house. Sarah was already halfway here with her arms filled with packages. A slight breeze rustled the branches, causing the sparkly pine cones that contained our wishes to sway from the limbs. Today, my son would face the harsh truth that not all wishes come true. Until then, he'd open his presents and think he was the luckiest boy in town.

"It's a bit breezy out there." Sarah shuffled through the door and shivered. She piled her gifts under the tree and hugged us one by one.

Tommy dispersed his handmade gifts with pride. Most of them he brought from New York. He'd decoupaged his picture on a tile and glazed over it to create a coaster for coffee. Under his name, he'd written "Good Morning." The gift he gave to me was perfect. It was a keychain with the biggest fake diamond ever.

"Oh, my God," I squealed. "You got me a diamond." There was nothing as wonderful as the look of a kid who knew he'd done well.

"Do you like it?"

I hugged him tightly. "It's super duper, buddy. The bestest ever."

He tore through his gifts like a Nor'easter. He hit hard and fast, leaving a trail of paper behind while he played with his new Legos and action figures.

Mom opened the new Keurig coffee pot I bought for her, and she looked excited.

"Do you mean to tell me that with the push of a button I can have a mocha or a tea on demand?"

"Yep." I tore through the box to show her the sample brews it included like hot chocolate and chai tea.

"It will be sad to say goodbye to the old pot, but out with the old and in with the new, they say." Proud was an understatement. My mom was moving forward with the velocity of a runaway freight train. If I didn't watch her carefully, I'd come to find her living in a smart house with every gadget known to man, but if that's the worst thing that happened, I was on board.

Sarah jumped up. "Oh, I almost forgot." She pulled two small boxes from her bag and handed one to Tommy and one to me. "These are from Beau."

Tommy held his to his nose like somehow it would bring him closer to Beau. I did the same but there wasn't a trace of him anywhere on the red, ribbon-wrapped cardboard.

"You first, Tommy."

Unlike the other gifts, Tommy didn't tear through the packaging to get inside. He took his time and untied the bow. When he lifted the cover, his eyes lit up. Inside was a guitar pick and note that said the old guitar was his.

Tears ran down my face. I was excited for my son to receive such a cherished gift, but also sad I'd have to relinquish the last bit of Beau I had. "It's upstairs in Mommy's room." I barely got the last word out before he raced away to find it.

"Open yours." Sarah put her arm around me and I wondered if what I'd find in the box would require the emotional support she was giving me. Like Tommy, I didn't rush through the experience. I relished the feeling of the red ribbon sliding between my fingers. I closed my eyes and imagined a different kind of Christmas—one ten years from now where Beau handed out presents to our mothers and our children. That would never be. I hoped that on the occasions he came back to visit, we could be friends.

When I slipped the top off the box, there was a single, old, rusty key. No note. No explanation.

"What is it?" My mom looked over my shoulder.

"It's a key, but I haven't got a clue to what." Sarah shrugged her shoulders and so did my mother. "He didn't tell you?"

Sarah shook her head. "No, he said you'd figure it out."

"When did you talk to him?"

"This morning, before I came over here. He called just before old man Swanson called about the house at the lake, which brings me to ask you for a favor."

"Sure, what do you need?"

"It seems someone left a light on in the house. Could you go and check it out? You still have the key, right?"

I felt embarrassed to not have returned the key last night. It was an oversight, or maybe I was just hanging on to the past for a little bit longer.

"I'll head over now if you guys can keep an eye on Tommy." I could hear him strumming his guitar upstairs.

"That's what grandmas do," they said in unison.

I didn't anticipate being back at the lake house so soon. When I parked the car, I went straight to the front door. Through the window, I could see the kitchen light on. I swear I turned it off, but obviously I didn't.

When the door popped open, I inhaled his scent. It was as if he were standing in front of me in his tight blue jeans and snug T-shirt. I listened with false hope that maybe he was here. Maybe he'd shown up for his mom and was waiting to surprise her. Stillness greeted me.

I walked through the house and nothing seemed out of order. The beds were made, the closets shut, the taps closed tight. Only the memory of Beau remained. I breathed him in once more before I locked up the house and walked to the end of the dock.

CHAPTER TWENTY-FIVE

BEAU

I tiptoed behind her. "You're trespassing, you know." She jumped a foot in the air and turned around to face me. She was a hot, beautiful mess. Her hair was pulled into a ponytail. She didn't have a bit of makeup on. Her sweatpants hung off her hips, and she was perfect.

"Beau. What are you doing here?"

"I told you I'd never leave you." I took a step forward, and she fell to her knees on the hard wooden dock.

"You have to. What about your contract? What about the band?"

"Haven't we made these mistakes before, Mandy? The contract was for three years. You're the rest of my life. Which do you think has more value?"

She rolled back to her bottom, and I took a seat in front of her. "I'm not worth what you'd give up."

"No, you're worth a hundred times more."

"Oh, Beau, you've made a mistake."

I grabbed her hands before she could bury her face in them. "It's a mistake if you don't love me."

"I do love you, that's why I let you go." She looked at her hands sitting on top of mine and a look of understanding crossed her face.

She was always too slow and like every other time I slapped the top of her hand, I brought it to my mouth for aftercare. My kisses rained over her knuckles.

"If you're going to be my wife, you're going to have to do two things."

Her eyes widened. "Your wife?"

I ignored her question and continued with my demands. "You're going to have to trust me to make good decisions when you don't." I gave her a what-were-you-thinking-look. "And you're going to have to get better at chicken."

"That's all you want?"

"No, baby, I want so much more, but I'll start with that," I pulled her into my lap and slanted my mouth over hers, "and this." The kiss started timid and turned torrid. Our tongues danced as our bodies melded together. It was a forever kiss, one that would be burned into our hearts. Unbreakable for all time. She clutched my shoulders like she'd never let go and that was a good thing because I'd never allow it.

"Let's go inside so I can make love to you."

"Oh, God," she groaned.

I pulled her up and lifted her into my arms and raced her inside. It took me about two point five seconds to get her naked and another second to bury myself deep inside her. I wasn't sure I'd ever want to live anywhere else but her body.

I stroked her with every ounce of love I possessed. "I love you, Mandy. This is forever." I pounded into her, hoping she'd remember those words the next time she decided to make choices for us. "You'll marry me, and we'll be a family." She nodded and moaned. I sucked in her nipple and she sucked in her breath. I could feel her tense. "Say it, Mandy. Say the word I want to hear." I reached between us and pulled the words from her.

"Yes. Yes. Yes," she screamed until the words softened into a whisper.

Her words caused a storm in me that couldn't be tamed. I shook and trembled over her body until everything I had to give this woman poured deep inside of her. She was the beginning and end for me. There would be no others.

Glistening in the afterglow of perfect lovemaking, she rolled to her side and walked her fingers up my chest until her palm laid over my thundering heart.

"What's going to happen now?"

I gripped her hand to my chest, refusing to let it go. She was my heart and her hand felt right there. Turning, I faced her. "I'm glad you asked." I kissed the tip of her nose and nipped at her swollen lips. "It just so happens that Rocco Piat wanted to work with BT and the Bads as much as we wanted to work with him. We renegotiated the deal. I took a small pay cut, but in the end, I came out ahead. I got the job and the girl."

"Do you have to be in California?" She sucked in

her cheek, and I could tell she was chewing her worry away.

"A couple days a month. That is until our studio is ready, then we can work from here, too. Did you know that Rocco has a place in Aspen?"

She pinched herself. "Nope, not dreaming." Then, she bolted upright. "Oh, my God, it's Christmas and I left my son with our mothers."

"No, you left our son with his grandmothers and besides the nice little sugar high he'll get, he'll be fine." I rolled from the bed and pulled on my jeans. "Ready to see your Christmas present?"

She looked at the crotch of my jeans. "Every perfect inch of it."

"Get dressed. We have things to do and wishes to grant."

We left her car in the driveway and climbed into the SUV. A side-glance at Mandy told me she was looking at life through a new lens. Her green eyes shone like flawless emeralds as I drove through town.

When I stopped at the old Grady place on Diamond Lane, she burst into tears.

"It's a diamond in the rough, baby, but it's your diamond." She flung herself across the center console and kissed me senseless.

"You bought this old house for me?"

"No, I bought it for us and our family."

She leaned back and gave me a come-hither look. "Do you know how many bedrooms this house has?"

"Yep, and I plan to fill every single one of them with a screaming little Tinsel." She reached into her pocket and pulled out the rusted key I gave her. "Shall we practice?"

We entered the rickety old house. It looked better on the inside than the outside. Mandy always had a way of seeing the good inside of things, including me. I took my shirt off and laid her back on the floor of the grand entry. This was our place and we'd christen it this Christmas with love.

"Beau," Tommy raced toward me. "You're back. I knew you'd come back." He lifted his arms, and I pulled him in for a big hug. I was late to the daddy date, and I hoped he'd allow me to hold him and hug him for years to come.

"I'm here, buddy. I'd never leave you."

"I knew it." A big grin took over his face. " If you left for good, who was going to teach me guitar? How was I going to get the fishing pole back?"

"We'll get it all figured out, okay? Go get the Grand-mas, it's pine cone time."

Annie came out with a basket in her arms and we plucked the decorated pine cones like apples from the tree. Everyone followed her into the house.

Stunned by the transformation, I said, "I like what you've done with the place."

She set down the basket and waved her hands around like a game show host. "It's a work in progress." She looked at Mandy with motherly love. "We started with a water theme, but it didn't go so well."

I pulled Mandy to my lap on the pink beanbag chair. "Oh, I don't know. I think you may be on to something." I nibbled on my girl's neck while *our* son handed out wishes.

The thing about pine cone wishes was, you weren't always sure who the wish came from or who it was for.

Mom started the event by pulling out the tiny paper tucked between two red, glittered scales.

"I wish everyone a merry Christmas."

We looked around the room and yelled, "granted." Then, we moved on to the next.

Mandy read the green glittered cone. "I want Beau to be my daddy." Everyone let out an "oh" before they yelled, "granted."

Annie read the next one. It was a multicolored thing of beauty. "I, Beau Tinsel, want to own Mandy's heart forever."

The only one who could grant that wish was Mandy, and she didn't hesitate to scream, "granted."

Tommy pulled the slip of paper from his pine cone. He studied the words before he spoke. "I want everyone to be happy."

"Granted."

I had the last pine cone, it sparkled gold in my hands. The little paper unfolded in my fingers and I read its inscription. "I want another grandchild as sweet as Tommy and as pretty as Mandy."

No one said a word. This wasn't a wish we could grant at this time.

Tommy broke the silence. "The thing about wishes is that they can come true anytime."

We exchanged looks with one another.

"I promise that I'll do my part to grant this wish."

Mandy raised her hand, "Me too."

Annie clapped her hands and shouted, "It's as good as granted."

And that's how we started our holiday as a family. We ate roasted chicken on a rickety Formica table and relaxed on a rainbow of beanbag chairs.

I tucked Tommy in with a song and left my guitar on Mandy's bed and unlocked her window. She clung to me as I kissed her goodnight. Little did she know, I was going as far as Mr. Peters' house to borrow the ladder.

Times Square was at capacity as Tommy and I stood in the wings of the stage, waiting for BT and the Bads to bring in the New Year.

Beau walked to the mic and silenced the crowd.

"This next song is dedicated to a girl I've loved since the day she was born." He looked at me and flagged me over.

I shook my head. I wasn't bright lights and big city. I was all about Beau and what happened between the sheets.

"Mandy, come out here." My face became bigger than life as every camera zoomed in on me. I was on display across Times Square and in hundreds of thousands of homes across the world. I was the envy of every woman who ever loved a rock star.

Gripping Tommy's hand, I inched my way to the center of the stage.

"Hold this for me will you?" He pressed a kiss to my lips and handed me the mic just before he dropped to his knees in front of our son. "Tommy Sawyer, you're the son I've always wanted, and if you'll have me, I'll be the best dad I can be." He whispered something into his ear and Tommy nodded.

Tommy reached for the mic, but before I'd give it to him, I looked to Beau for guidance. When he nodded, I relinquished it.

"Hi." The thousands of bodies surrounding us absorbed his little voice.

"A little louder, buddy." Beau gave him an encouraging pat on the back.

"Hi," Tommy repeated. This time, the world could hear him. "My name is Tommy Sawyer. I know it was a mean mommy name, but my new daddy asked me to be a Tinsel and I said yes." The crowd erupted into applause.

Beau took the microphone and looked at the crowd. "In about ten years, you better be watching for Tommy Sawyer-Tinsel. The kid is already shredding."

The band began to play a song I didn't recognize. I slipped my hand over Tommy's and tried to slink off the stage. "Oh no, you don't." Beau held me in place, turned toward me, and sang his new release. "My Forever." At the end of the song, he took a knee again and in front of the world, Beau Tinsel proposed to me. Seconds later, the ball dropped, confetti flew, and good wishes rang out while I brought the new year in with my family —my future husband and son.

The house would take a year to renovate so we stayed at the cabin and worked on Mom's wish. It took us forty-four days, but on Valentine's Day, we stood on the doorstep of Mom's renovated house. When she opened the door, I held up the positive pregnancy test and we all yelled, "granted."

GET A FREE BOOK.

Go to www.authorkellycollins.com

ABOUT THE AUTHOR

International bestselling author of more than thirty novels, Kelly Collins writes with the intention of keeping love alive. Always a romantic, she blends real-life events with her vivid imagination to create characters and stories that lovers of contemporary romance, new adult, and romantic suspense will return to again and again.

For More Information
www.authorkellycollins.com
kelly@authorkellycollins.com